Since I arrived in England, so much has happened. Most of it was like a bad dream. I know it all started in Joburg when I killed Philemon Majodena, or maybe even earlier than that, when I was born into my white skin. But when I got to this country, I thought all the blood I spilled was left behind. No way, man! That trouble followed me here like a pack of starving hyenas.

It was like Macbeth. *Except that it was black blood on my fifteen-year-old white hands. And no amount of washing with Lux soap could get it out.*

"What will haunt readers is the universal moral issue, the connection made between this ordinary family and the ordinary people who went along with slavery and with the Holocaust." —*Booklist*

No Tigers in Africa

A NOVEL BY
Norman Silver

PUFFIN BOOKS

PUFFIN BOOKS

Published by the Penguin Group

Penguin Books USA Inc., 375 Hudson Street, New York, New York 10014, U.S.A.

Penguin Books Ltd, 27 Wrights Lane, London W8 5TZ, England

Penguin Books Australia Ltd, Ringwood, Victoria, Australia

Penguin Books Canada Ltd, 10 Alcorn Avenue, Toronto, Ontario, Canada M4V 3B2

Penguin Books (N.Z.) Ltd, 182-190 Wairau Road, Auckland 10, New Zealand

Penguin Books Ltd, Registered Offices: Harmondsworth, Middlesex, England

First published in Great Britain by Faber and Faber Limited, 1990

First published in the United States of America by Dutton Children's Books,

a division of Penguin Books USA Inc., 1992

Published in Puffin Books, 1994

1 3 5 7 9 10 8 6 4 2

THE LIBRARY OF CONGRESS HAS CATALOGED THE DUTTON CHILDREN'S BOOKS EDITION AS FOLLOWS:

Silver, Norman.

No Tigers in Africa / by Norman Silver.—1st American ed. p. cm.

Summary: Newly arrived in England from South Africa,

a fifteen-year-old's family deteriorates as the

effects of living under apartheid take a toll on every

aspect of the family members' lives.

ISBN 0-525-44733-4

[1. Family problems—Fiction. 2. South Africa—Fiction.

3. England—Fiction. 4. Apartheid—South Africa—Fiction.

5. Moving, Household—Fiction.] I. Title.

PZ7.S585736No 1992 91-29121 [Fic]—dc20 CIP AC

Puffin Books ISBN 0-14-036935-X

Set in the United States of America

The characters and events described in this book are fictions. I would like to be able to say that the South Africa described, with its racial policy of apartheid, is a fiction too. But it is all too real.

It was Bala's suggestion that I write this book. He said it would be like a laxative for me—in other words, it would help to get all the crap out. So here it all comes, and don't expect it to smell sweet.

Some of the things I'm going to tell you about myself really shame me. It hurts to bring these things out into the open. I used to think that there are some things that a person does under their own blanket that should never be told in the light of day. But Bala didn't agree. He would sniff out any piece of rot in a person and put it on the table to be examined. He firmly believes that only when the rot's out then life can begin to flow.

Chapter 1

Since I arrived in England, so much has happened. Most of it was like a bad dream. I know it all started in Joburg when I killed Philemon Majodena, or maybe even earlier than that, when I was born into my white skin. But when I got to this country, I thought all the blood I spilled was left behind. No way, man! That trouble followed me here like a pack of starving hyenas.

It was like *Macbeth*. Except that it was black blood on my fifteen-year-old white hands. And no amount of washing with Lux soap could get it out.

I tell you, when I got here, those hyenas started

yowling. I could hear their snarls and even their breath, they came so close. They chased me right to death's door, and I was standing there knocking like mad. You know, I knocked so loudly they nearly let me in. I could actually hear footsteps on the other side of the door. 'Strues God, they nearly let me in. And I don't think they were planning on giving me a good welcome. I think it would have been like coming to England, bladdy freezing and no one to welcome us.

From the sky we couldn't even see England. When the pilot said, "Fasten your seat belts, Heathrow ahead," I couldn't believe it. There were just dark clouds all around us—and it was already seven o'clock in the morning. Jeez, it was dark. When we left Jan Smuts Airport the evening before, it was a fantastic Joburg summer day—blue sky and hot. I don't mean it was especially fantastic. No way! Most Joburg summer days are like that. Of course, it clouds over most afternoons, but only for an hour at the most, and then it rains like hell, and there's forked lightning and thunderblasts, but then it gets it all out of its system, the sun comes out again, and everyone jumps back in the swimming pool.

Talk about Adam and Eve leaving paradise! At least when they left the Garden of Eden, they went to a hot place. But maybe that's because they only ate an apple. That was their sin. But I had the blood of an African boy on my hands, and that's a different kettle of fish.

I couldn't believe it when I stepped off that plane. It was pitch dark, except for electric lights shining, and it was so cold I could see my own breath coming out of my own mouth in a misty cloud.

To tell you the truth, I still haven't gotten used to the cold. I mean, it's summer here now. August. Out of the window here at the Villa, I can see some trees full of green leaves. But the sun is just like a copper coin in the sky—it doesn't give off any heat. English people call this summer. But I'm still cold. There haven't been more than a dozen days that I would call hot. I hardly ever wear shorts. Still, maybe I'll get used to the climate if my blood thickens or something. I shouldn't complain, really. I bet it would have been colder behind death's door.

Anyway, to go back to the welcome we got in England. There wasn't one. Nobody met us at Heathrow. And we didn't expect anyone either. The only people we knew of in this country were Uncle Colin and Aunt Noreen and their family. But they live in York or somewhere, and we didn't expect them to come and meet us. My ma's probably got relations somewhere, but who knows where? We looked in the phone book and there were lots of Woolfs—that was her maiden name—and we couldn't phone them all and ask if they knew Ma's old man forty years ago.

So we took the train to Bristol. There was me and my ma and my old man and my sister Stelly (her real name's Estelle). My older sister Lynette is now in Australia, lucky thing! But Oupa was with us. That's Afrikaans for "grandfather." We're not an Afrikaans family, really; we're English-speaking, but sometimes we use a few words from Afrikaans, which is the other white language.

Actually, we're not properly English like English people who live in England. Only my ma's old man came from England. Her ma was German. My old man's parents came from Gdansk, which is in Poland, I think. My grandparents all died a while ago, except for Oupa, who came with us to England.

So you see I'm half Polish, a quarter German, and just one quarter proper English. I think that quarter helped a lot to get my family into England. But anyway, like I was saying, we're an English-speaking family even though I call my grandfather Oupa.

When we got to Bristol, we lived in a guesthouse for two weeks, and then in a rented apartment. It was really dingy. I can't tell you how dingy Bristol looked after Joburg. Let's just put it this way: Joburg is really modern. And in summer the roads are lined with jacarandas—both sides of the street usually. A jacaranda is a big tree with beautiful blue flowers. The whole tree just goes blue in summer, and it's fantastic until it drops its flowers. Then as the car wheels drive over them, it's snap, crackle, pop. Jeez, but it can also be a mess.

We used to have this swimming pool under a row of jacaranda trees. It was okay until the flowers dropped off, but then it was trouble. The flowers dropped in the swimming pool, and Alfred—that's our African garden boy—used to have to scoop the flowers off the surface with a big, round mesh thing every day. If he missed a day, the flowers sank to the bottom and turned brown and rotted and then turned green. And by that time it had turned to algae, and it was a heck of a job to get rid of it off the sides with our lousy filter machine. The trouble was, our swimming pool was quite old because we weren't such a rich family by Joburg standards.

At the beginning of the hot season every year, the pool had to be cleaned out. Every year it was the same. The machine pumped out most of the water, but it couldn't pump out the last few hundred gallons, I don't know why. And that last bit was usually slimy green, and in it there were live frogs jumping or dead frogs floating.

Alfred used to do the emptying job with a bucket. He used to fill one bucket, then walk all the way up the empty pool to the shallow end and then up through the baby pool, and tip the water out in the garden. Then he'd walk all the way back down again and fill another bucket.

"Alfred, why you so stupid?" I used to ask him. "Why don't you tie a rope around the bucket and just throw it in and then pull it up? It's much quicker. Come up here, I'll show you how to do it."

And when I showed him, it was much quicker, and you didn't have to stand barefoot in the slimy green water. But every year he started off the same way, and every year I had to come and tie the rope to the bucket for him. He knew how to make a four-hour job last four days, that's for sure.

The house we bought in Bristol didn't have a swimming pool—no chance. The money my parents brought out from South Africa was only enough to get us this thing they call a terraced. I've never seen a house like that before—it was joined to the neighbors on either side! No wonder all the streets in England look like the houses have been squashed together. I've seen blocks of apartments where I suppose you could say the apartments are joined to each other. But joined-up houses, never. Anyway, I got used to it after a few months. It wasn't so bad. You couldn't really hear the neighbors like I first thought.

Oupa didn't like the house from the first moment. He got the room on the ground level because he wasn't so good on steps. But his main problem was he kept forgetting where his room was. If he'd been out of his room for more than ten minutes, he couldn't find it again.

Stelly got the best room, the one in the attic. At least it had a bit of a view of a few bushes. My room looked over the street, and it was just nonstop traffic all day. When I think of my bedroom in Joburg, it still makes me feel funny. It was so nice. Outside the window was a Lady of Spain bush. That's the bush with massive red trumpet flowers, and you pull off the petals one by one and sing "Lady of Spain, I adore you; pull down your broeks, I'll explore you." Broeks are pants, and by the time all the petals are pulled off, the whole inside of the flower is just naked. And beyond the Lady of Spain you could see two flat palm trees, the pond overgrown with reeds, and the whole driveway of jacarandas. It was lekker. That's another Afrikaans word, and I use it a lot. It means "nice."

The house in Bristol was better than the guesthouse or the apartment, that's for sure. There was more space for everyone. But it didn't stop the arguing between my old man and my ma. Every night I heard them going at it.

"We should never have moved, man," my ma would scream. "You must have been out of your mind to sell the business."

"I'm telling you it was downhill all the way," my old man would say. "Bankruptcy road. And all those bombs and riots. The signs were there for us, and we were lucky to get out of it."

"You only think of yourself, number one, big shot. You never think of me. I had to leave all my friends behind."

"What do you want of me, woman? You bladdy deaf or something? You got no business sense. We got out of that place just in time. The whole country's going to explode any day."

At this point, my ma would be crying. She doesn't know much about business, that's true, but she's got a university degree in art. In Joburg she used to do all this charity work, and one thing she did was help out this gallery place for black artists. My old man always heaped scorn on her about art and never went with her to exhibitions or anything.

Sometimes after a row my old man would try and make up to my ma. He'd comb his long fingers through her blonde hair and smile his handsome moustache smile and say, "It'll work out okay; you'll see." But Ma didn't think he looked so handsome after those rows, and he didn't sound very confident either, and my ma's hair wasn't really blonde. It was all dyed, and you could see the brown roots showing through if you looked closely.

I honestly think the only person who was not depressed about the move was Stelly. She was only seven and looked at everything new with those wide eyes of hers. Everyone always used to say how cute Stelly was with her blonde hair—which wasn't dyed —and her wide eyes and the freckles on her nose and under her eyes. Being that age, things like moving country don't affect you so badly. There's a lot of water under the bridge between seven and fifteen, as she will find out one day.

When you move country at fifteen, the most difficult thing is friends. I can't begin to tell you how much I missed my old pals. We had a great bunch. There was Gav, who was the loudest one and boasted the most. Then there was Nobby, who was so pimply you couldn't see the skin between his acne. And Joel, who was fantastic at sports. (He held the school record for high jump and hundred meters—the under-fifteen, I mean.) And there was me, Selly, the brainy one, they called me. You might think it's funny that my sister's called Stelly and I'm called Selly, but that's not my parents' fault. She's actually Estelle and I'm Selwyn, which doesn't sound so crazy, but when they're shortened to Selly and Stelly, I know it sounds a bit weird. Lynette never had a short name. I can't imagine her being called Lynne or Nettie. I suppose that's because she was always much older than me and now she's a married woman.

Our bunch used to hang out everywhere together. We used to go to Hillbrow for laughs mostly, or parties, and at school we used to stick together. Ag,

I miss those guys. Sorry, I know I say "ag" a lot. It sounds like the Germans when they say "ach," but at this Bristol school they laughed when I said "ag."

It's so different over here. I didn't have one good friend at school. They were okay, but they didn't laugh when I made jokes, and most of the time they said "Wha?" when I spoke, 'cause they couldn't understand my way of talking. I didn't even think I had an accent until I came to this country and then I found out.

I couldn't understand them half the time either. And it wasn't just the nonwhites, so you mustn't think I was prejudiced about that 'cause I wasn't.

When I first went to that school, it was halfway through their school year. They begin in September—it's really crazy. In South Africa, school begins in January, which makes more sense, doesn't it? It was January when I came to Bristol, but they were already halfway through their work, and they all had their own friends. The teacher said this boy, Lloyd, should show me around. He was okay, Lloyd. I didn't mind that he was black at all. In fact, I tried extra hard to be nice to him, but I had terrible trouble understanding his way of speaking.

"Oy thart you'd be girt bluck, mun, you bein' from Sote Ahfrica."

The only word I recognized was *Ahfrica*.

There was quite a mixture of kids in my class. There were eight blacks and four Indians and a mixture of twenty-one white kids, but one of them came from Newcastle, and I couldn't understand him at all.

There was one boy whose name is Jeff who, I must admit, tried to be friendly. He got me to come to soccer practice, and he helped me in math. See, the thing is, we were doing different work in Joburg, so they thought I was a bit stupid at first. We did lots of South African history, about Jan van Riebeek and the wars with the Xhosas and the Zulus and the Matabeles and the Great Trek and all that stuff that they don't do here. And we did cadets, which is marching up and down all morning in a khaki uniform. (That's one thing I used to hate, 'cause I'm a nonviolent person. I never wanted to do any army service in South Africa and, thank goodness, now I won't have to. Poor old Gav and Nobby and Joel. They'll probably have to go and fight up on the borders.) We also did Afrikaans, which they don't do here, and we did Latin, but they do French here, and we didn't do the kind of math they do here, with practical problems and all that. But Jeff helped me, and he could see I wasn't stupid. Jeff was okay to me until our discussion about apartheid. Then he went off the deep end.

He knew a bit about apartheid, which made a change. The other kids in our class thought South Africa was all the land at the bottom of Africa, and, like Lloyd, they thought I'd be black and that there were lions walking around Joburg. But Jeff knew a bit. I didn't know at the time, but I've found out since, that Jeff's parents are members of Anti-Apartheid. He mixes a lot with kids of all races.

Anyway, we had this discussion about apartheid, which I don't agree with—no way—though I've never taken much interest in politics. He said *all* the people of South Africa should have a vote.

"No, you don't know what it's like there," I said. "Most black people don't know what voting's about."

"But all people are the same," Jeff said. "They should mix together and have the same rights."

"No, people are all different," I said. "They shouldn't have to be mixed together in a Mixmaster if they don't want it."

"But don't you think all people are equal?" he asked.

"Of course," I said. "You think I'm in favor of apartheid? My family votes for change. Honestly. But most of the blacks aren't educated enough to have a proper vote. They should only be allowed to elect their own black leaders and leave the whites to vote in the government."

Jeez, that made him wild. He looked at me like I was a criminal. And he wouldn't speak to me after that, even when I tried to tell him that he didn't understand. He should have met Alfred, I thought, then he would have known what I meant. Or that African we asked directions from in the Drakensberg Mountains.

I explained to Jeff about it. My whole family in our car was driving along this gravel road for hours, and we got lost. Then we saw this African chap walking on the side of the road toward us. So my old man slowed down.

"Where does this road go?" my old man asked him.

"That way!" the African says, pointing back down the road, and then walked on again.

He wouldn't have known about voting, that's for sure. But Jeff didn't agree.

The afternoon of that discussion was soccer practice, and Jeff was horrible to me all the way through. He wouldn't have me on his team, and he tackled me viciously and he kept shouting, "Wasn't that off side?" whenever I got into a good position to score.

Mr. Wilson wasn't much help either. He kept on agreeing with Jeff and blowing his whistle against me for off side. Jeez, it made me mad. I don't mean only mad cross; I mean mad crazy also. About halfway through the game, my brain was burning up, if you know what I mean. Instead of using up energy on the field, it was using me up, and just after half time I flipped out. I got fouled again, and my shins got bruised. That was the last straw. The next time the ball came near me, I picked it up in my hands and started to run for the opposition line. Man, I really thought I was doing well! I got to the line in good style and dived over for a try. The only shame was that the ball was round and not oval like a rugby ball.

"Soccer's crap!" I shouted out. "It's only for moffies!" They probably didn't understand me, 'cause *moffie* is Afrikaans slang for "transvestite."

Jeff and a few others came running toward me like they wanted to teach me a lesson about soccer that I'd never forget. But I ran like hell. My head was spinning with bad thoughts. If they caught me, maybe they'd kill me or something.

I ran off the field, over the wire fence, and into the road. I threw the ball over a wall into someone's front garden. My studs clanked along the road, so I pulled off my boots and ran in my socks.

For a while I didn't know where to run to. I wanted to run home to Joburg, to my room looking out on the Lady of Spain and the pond and the palm trees and the jacarandas.

I ran along, even though no one was chasing me anymore, and I passed an imaginary rugby ball to my fullback. I always played wing 'cause I'm quite fast for my age. Fast and quite strong. My team-mates used to call me Mighty Bullet. They also used to call me the Wintergreen Boy 'cause I used to rub this stuff called Deep Heat into all my muscles before a game. It used to feel good, and it smelled of Wick's Bubble Gum. The only trouble was if you got it on your balls or your poep, it burned like hell. I'm sure I don't have to tell you what a poep is, but I'll tell you it's got the sound of *oo* in *book*.

Rugby was the second-best thing in my life in Joburg. I won't tell you now what the best thing was. I'll surprise you later. But rugby was definitely second best.

I wasn't brilliant at it like my pal Joel, but I played hard. I tackled hard, I ran hard, and I fell hard. Once when our headmaster was watching the game, I knocked out two teeth of the opposing wing's mouth with the top of my head. It was a massive tackle. You might think I'd get in trouble for hurting someone on the field. Not at all. After the match, the headmaster himself came up to me.

"You showed a lot of spirit in that game, Lewis." (Lewis is my surname, but in Poland it was Lubowski or something like that. My oupa changed his name when he went to South Africa.)

I felt really proud of myself. "Ja, thanks, Mr. Tarling."

"Keep it up, boy," he said.

My ambition in life was to get rugby colors from the school. As I ran along that Bristol street, I just wanted to be playing for my old school, with my headmaster watching, so that he would award me colors.

When I got home, my ma was not pleased.

"What do you think I am?" she said. "Matilda?"

Matilda used to be our African servant girl in Joburg.

"I'm not your slave!" my ma said. "You can go and wash those socks yourself! I haven't got a girl to do these things here!"

That was the same day Oupa went missing for the first time.

Just before six o'clock, my old man came home from work. We were all just about to sit down for dinner when it suddenly became apparent that Oupa wasn't there. We searched the house top to bottom, but he'd disappeared.

"Didn't you see him leave the house?"

My old man was cross with my ma. His bony hands were waving all over the place—it was a habit whenever he was cross.

"What else did you have to do here all day? You

should have kept an eye on him. He's not that well, you know."

"I can't spend my life looking after your father," my ma answered. "It was your idea to bring him. He'd have been much better off at the old-age home."

"You've no feelings, Helen."

"You should talk about feelings," my ma said. "You don't even know what they are."

My old man and I went looking for him in the car. It was an old Renault, nothing like the Ford automatic we had in Joburg.

Up and down the streets we drove, peering into the darkness for Oupa. Over one hour we spent driving, stopping in at the house every now and again to see if he'd returned. But there was no sign of him. It was freezing outside, enough to make an old man's knee joints and brain freeze solid.

"He'll die if he's outside in this," my old man said. I knew it was true.

When there was still no sign of him at seven o'clock, my old man said, "Better contact the police, I suppose."

We gave the police a description, but it wasn't needed that time. When we got home, Oupa was there. He'd just arrived. He had gotten lost somewhere in Redland and had simply knocked on the front door of some house. Whoever answered was kind enough to ask Oupa to search his pockets for identification. Fortunately, they found a letter on him and brought him back home. (It was actually a letter addressed to my old man that he thought had never arrived.)

"Where've you been, Pa?" my old man asked him.

"Looking for Fanny," he said. Fanny was his wife, who had died five years earlier.

"Don't you know Fanny died five years ago? We're in Bristol. In England."

"Here isn't Joburg?" he asked.

I felt so sorry for Oupa. Here I was feeling lost in this country, and there he was doubly lost 'cause he had made two country moves in his life.

"Look at your jacket, Pa. Don't you remember?"

My old man pointed to a tear in Oupa's jacket, which had been cut by the rabbi at Fanny's funeral. It's a Jewish custom, I think, to remind you that you're sad. I told you my family was half Polish, quarter German, quarter English. They're also Jewish, though my ma doesn't believe in any of it.

I think most people throw away their jackets once they've been cut like that, but not Oupa. About six months after the funeral, I found him at the boarding house where he lived in Berea, sewing up the rip. He wasn't very good at sewing, but the rip wasn't so noticeable anymore after that.

Oupa looked at the rip in his jacket like it was in a far-off dream. I thought maybe he would say something, but he didn't. He started shaking instead. Maybe it was sadness; maybe it was the shock of recognizing something; maybe it was the cold.

My old man wrapped him in a blanket, sat him by the radiator, and gave him a whisky. He looked really worn out, and his cheeks were covered with prickly silver stubble. Oupa's eyes were blue as a Jo-burg sky, but they looked like they were staring into other worlds. Maybe he could hear footsteps on the other side of death's door.

Like I said, that was the first of about five similar journeys Oupa went on in those first months we lived in Bristol.

And after his fifth journey, death's door did open.

Chapter 2

The days after I played rugby with the soccer ball were really terrible at school. Someone pinned this note on the wall saying *Keep South Africans out of sport!* and nobody spoke to me. Even the teachers looked at me like I was from another planet, which I was almost. Mr. Wilson must have told them all that I was a bit of a doos. That's Afrikaans, by the way, for "a cardboard box," but if you call someone that, you probably mean they're an idiot. To tell the truth, I was even worried that *I* was becoming a doos.

In Joburg I was considered brainy by my pals and by my teachers, but at this school I couldn't do anything right. Math I found difficult, French I found impossible, and European history really boring. And in English, which I'd always been good at, I suddenly found myself very embarrassed. Each time I was asked to read, everyone said, "Wha? Wha's he saying?"

Talking about English lessons has reminded me that I said rugby was my second-best thing in the world. Well, now I'm going to tell you what my best thing is. But you mustn't laugh. Because, 'strues bob, I'd moerra anyone who laughs at me. And *moerra,* if you don't know, means "to beat the living daylights out of someone."

My very best things is—and it's strange because you wouldn't think someone whose second-best thing is rugby would have this for a best thing—my very best thing is poetry. There, now you know. Rugby and poetry, that's a good combination, hey?

I've always read a lot of poetry. And at home in Joburg I've got—ag, now that's stupid of me to say *got*—I mean I used to have thousands of books of poetry. Maybe not thousands, but a lot. I'll tell you where I got them, but don't say too much about this to anyone. I stole them. Ja, I stole them all, man. Every single one. Except for one or two that I paid for out of my own pocket money. I was an expert thief. I could go into any bookshop in Joburg, even the ones with store detectives and video cameras, and come out with two or three books, usually poetry. In two years I must have stolen about a thousand rands' worth, I should think. You know how I did it? Under my jersey, as simple as that. Or do you call a jersey a sweater? I can't remember. You just pretend you're reading, but actually you're holding two books, the one you're going to rip off and the one you're pretending to read. Then you sort of lean over and slip it under your jersey and sort of halfway down into your pants. It's a bit difficult to walk out of the shop like that, but you get used to it. Stealing books was more of a winter activity for me because in summer I never wore jerseys.

Some people think I must be a split personality to like poetry and rugby, but I don't feel split. That's just me. I like reading poetry, and I also write a lot of poems myself, mainly after two o'clock in the morning. I don't let peole see them usually, because they're private. Should I tell you why I like poetry so much? Because poetry is written with a pen that's got gold ink in it. Do you know what I mean? I always imagine the poem I am reading was written in a workshop deep underground. There's machinery everywhere, like a gold mine, and the poet drills into the rock face to get out the valuable stuff he needs. And these rocks with their gold veins are collected together in huge vats and put into furnaces, which are burning at fantastically hot temperatures. When the vats come out of the furnace, they contain a liquid gold mixture. The poet pours the mixture into inkwells on his desk, and he fills up his pen while the mixture is still hissing and steaming.

That's why I like poetry so much, because some other parts of life are written with a shit-stick.

Oupa's funeral was really pathetic. I mean, if he had died in Joburg, there would have been hundreds of mourners. I don't mean people who are sad because of his passing, but I just mean people who come to a funeral. Because in Joburg you meet family you didn't even know you had until the day of the funeral. They turn up from far and wide, and they all look into your eyes for a brief moment as if you were their dearest friend and they shake your hand with heartfelt sympathy and they say, "Long life! We wish you a long life!" And then you don't see them again until the next funeral or wedding.

Stelly wasn't allowed to go to the funeral and was sent off to school, lucky thing. I've always hated cemeteries, but I had to go. Apart from my old man and my ma and me, the only other family there were Uncle Colin and Aunt Noreen. Actually I didn't know them, not really. I'd never met them before. But they are my ma's cousins. They both came up to me, looked into my eyes for a split second, shook my hand, and said, "Long life, Selwyn!" Then they did the same to my ma and my old man.

There were four other people there that my ma had made friends with since arriving in Bristol. My ma was always good at making friends. She's got a knack for it, if you know what I mean. In Joburg she was such a socializer. Apart from charity work and helping black artists, she played bridge and especially tennis and went to women's groups, and you name it, she used to do it if it meant mixing with people. She never worked, my ma, because before my old man made his money in the wholesale business, he was a director for a food company, so my ma was always a lady of leisure.

Anyway, these four people hardly knew my oupa. Maybe they saw him a few times or said hello to him, but they didn't really know him at all. Strangers they were to him really. But I suppose they came out of sympathy for my parents. I could understand Ginny coming because at least she's South African, even though she didn't know us in South Africa. Ma met her through a woman at Stelly's school who said she knew another South African living in Bristol. But I didn't know why her daughter Rosalie had to come. She was about my age, and she had visited us once or twice before, but to tell you the truth, I didn't get up the nerve to talk to her when she came. I must admit Rosalie tried to talk to me, and she seemed not too bad. I decided maybe next time she came I would talk to her. Anyway, they both came up to me and my family to shake hands. They didn't say "Long life!" or anything because they weren't Jewish.

But the other two people had me foxed. They were a black couple my ma met at the Sports Center. The first time I saw them with my ma, I thought maybe one of them was a black artist who needed some encouragement. Anyway, I didn't know why they came 'cause Oupa could only have met them once or twice. But I suppose, now we're in England, it's okay to have black people at funerals. There was a black person at Ouma Fanny's funeral, but it was only her servant girl, Gladys.

These two black people were very polite to me. They said, "Sorry about your sad loss," which I thought was a better thing to say than "Long life!" They shook hands with my ma and my old man also and said something to each of them that I didn't hear, and then I saw the black man do something I'd never seen before in my life. He actually put his cheek against my ma's cheek, like you sometimes see Russians, or is it French people, doing in films.

In Jewish custom, you have to have ten males over the age of thirteen before you can have a funeral. I mean ten live males. Usually that's no problem because most people have more than ten male mourners at their funeral. But Oupa didn't. There was only my old man, me, Uncle Colin, the black man (and I wasn't too sure if he counted—don't get me wrong, I mean just in Jewish custom, did it count?), the rabbi, and a man in a black suit next to the rabbi who had helped steer the coffin to the graveside. That makes a total of six males. The rabbi spoke to the man in the black suit, who went off and soon returned with four other Jewish gentlemen, and the funeral began. I don't know where those four came from, but I had the feeling they were paid to be mourners (I may be wrong on that, I don't know).

It was so cold that everyone there just wanted it to be over so that they could go back indoors and have a cup of tea. I bet Oupa had no idea his body was going to be laid in a cold-storage grave in England. My old man used to have a cold storage at the warehouse. It was the size of a big room, with a massive, thick door, and stacked to the roof with foodstuffs. Yirra! I wouldn't have liked to be locked in there even for half an hour. But Oupa had no choice. It was eternity in the cold storage for him.

Nobody cried for Oupa. At one funeral I had to go to in Joburg, for Ivor Sherman, who died in a traffic accident, everybody was howling. His wife and daughters were hysterical and flinging themselves on the ground every few moments. It was a terrible tragedy. But nobody cried for Oupa. Not even me. And I loved Oupa. I think in England the tear ducts are all frozen.

Of all my grandparents, Oupa gave me the most love, even when my other grandparents were alive. I don't know why. I was his first grandson, and I think that was important to him. And my name is quite similar to his. His name was Solomon, though everyone who knew him back in Joburg called him Solly. And I'm Selly; see what I mean? I wasn't named after him because my old man said that would have been unlucky. I think the names are quite close. But the physical resemblance was even closer. The one photo my family's got of him as a young boy back in Poland shows a tangle of blond hair just like I had when I was young and a triangular nose exactly like mine. But now, of course, my hair has gone brown, and Oupa's hair was white ever since I can remember.

People close to our family sometimes used to remark on the resemblance between us.

"Isn't Selly just like Oupa Solly?"

I read somewhere that there's a tribe who thinks that the spirit of the grandfather is born in the grandchild. I reckon that could be true. Except I don't know why there were two of us for such a long time. But now there's only one, so there's no need to ponder that problem.

We used to have great times together. During school holidays he used to stay with us. And he used to make me read him all sorts of things. He couldn't read any English, so he used to get me to read to him. About anything. We used to read encyclopedias together—not whole ones, just bits that interested him, like the lives of famous people like Tolstoy or Frederick Chopin, or exotic places like Java or Martinique. I think he wouldn't have chosen to die in England.

He once told me that he was helped to leave Poland by an officer in the army, who gave him money to buy a ship's passage. Jews were being persecuted at that time, and he was lucky to reach South Africa, where he could start a new life. He did well in his new country, that's for sure, because he lent my father the money to buy the wholesale business.

As I stood at his funeral, I was supposed to be starting a new life. But all I could see was a grave, with a body being lowered into it. I wasn't so sure that he had passed on his spirit to me. I didn't feel that much spirit within myself at all. I felt terrible, like something in me was dying. And I hated being in that cemetery.

Strange. I've always been afraid of cemeteries and dead bodies. Morbidly afraid, I would say. Poep-scared!

Whenever we used to drive past a cemetery, I

27

would duck in the backseat of the car. Nobody else ever knew about my fear. I wouldn't have dreamed of telling anyone. But for about two or three years, from about seven till ten years of age, I always ducked when we drove past cemeteries. I knew where they all were in Joburg, and I ducked well in advance and only surfaced after we had passed.

It started when Aunt Celia died of cancer. (She was my best friend's ma, and she was only twenty-nine at the time.) The night she died I dreamed of tigers—huge tigers, maneaters—stalking through the garden near the pond that was overgrown with reeds. My parents let me sleep in their bed that night, and my old man got out the same encyclopedia I used to read to Oupa and he read to me that there are no tigers in Africa. Well, tell that to whoever is directing my dreams! I've dreamed about huge, stalking tigers for seven years, and I'll tell you something else: They stalked me in Africa and they're stalking me in England. They scare the shit out of me, but they're so mysterious and awesome I don't think I'll ever stop dreaming about them.

It's like that poem of Blake's about the tigers burning in the night, and which immortal hand or eye could have created a beast as magnificent as a tiger. That's why I include Blake in my all-time favorite poets. He had the same dreams as me.

The day after Oupa's funeral I skipped school. I didn't tell anyone. I just walked and walked and landed up in Clifton near the suspension bridge. Don't get me wrong; I'm not saying I was thinking of jumping off it or anything. Those sorts of feelings came later. No, I actually found it very beautiful. That was the first place in England I ever liked. I sat looking down into the gorge for hours and hours.

I didn't speak to anyone. I didn't feel like speaking. I was silent. For the whole day. Even when I went home that afternoon, pretending I'd been at school, I just went straight to my room and lay down. Silent. Silent. I didn't want to disturb the things in my head. There was a wave of pressure somewhere in there, deep inside, in a place I only half knew about, the place where the tigers prowled, a wave of pressure that was building up like the waves at Durban that the surfers catch, huge rollers, a wave of energy, power, rage, fear, which could toss a surfer aside like a useless cork, a wave that could drag you under the sea, never to rise again (that happened to quite a few surfers at Durban), but if you caught that wave correctly, it would give you the ride of your life. That's why I was silent. I wanted to catch that wave and not be drowned by it. But I knew if I mistimed it, that would be overs-cadovers for me.

I was silent. But I also went for a Coke in this place in the antiques market where trendies hang out. And nobody bugged me there. They just let me sit silently. And no one asked why I wasn't in school.

That was the first of my silences, and they got worse after that, and people must have thought I was going mad, and maybe they were right.

The day after that first silence I was talking again, to my family at any rate. But at school I'd have done just as well to remain silent. Nobody hardly spoke to me.

Except for John Patel. He was an Indian boy, I think a Hindu, and in Joburg he wouldn't have been allowed in my school because those schools were for whites only. I don't know why he spoke to me because he wasn't very nice to me, and anyway, I still couldn't understand him properly.

He said why didn't I go to another school. I wanted to tell him that in South Africa, if an Indian boy used that tone of voice with a white person, then he was tired of living. But instead, I said, "What business is it of yours?"

"I am only asking," he said. "You don't have to say. Nobody seems to be liking you here very much."

I turned away from him. I didn't need an Indian boy to tell me that—not that I felt prejudiced or anything. I wouldn't have liked it if a white boy had said it either.

But I tell you I got a shock behind the bicycle stand that day. I was walking there to be alone when I came across Lloyd, the black boy, with Donna Preston. Jeez, that gave me a feeling all the way up my spine that I can't explain. Donna's a good-looking white girl, and I couldn't understand her behavior. She was smooching with Lloyd—honestly, her lips right up against his. I thought, God, they're in for such trouble, those guys. They're going to be locked away for abnormal behavior. But I couldn't stop myself from staring and staring and staring.

Then, when the tremors up my back subsided, I

realized this was okay in England. Jeez, but it made me feel uncomfortable. I kept thinking to myself that I wasn't a racist or anything, but some things just happen in your body without control, like tremors going up your back. And I didn't ask for that to happen when I saw them smooching.

In the meantime, I can tell you that Lloyd was damned annoyed with me for staring at him and Donna.

"Piss off," he said to me, in English I could understand.

I went back to the classroom. Mrs. Carter told us to get out our *Macbeth*s. That's our Shakespeare this year. But Macbeth was getting on my nerves. Since he murdered the king, he was seeing ghosts left, right, and center, and his mind was full of scorpions, and Lady Macbeth was going off her rocker, sleep-walking and washing her hands over and over to get rid of the blood. And I knew Macbeth was going to get his head chopped off at the end of the play.

Anyway, Mrs. Carter wanted me to read one of the parts, but I went white when she asked me, I mean pale, and I felt faint. The blood seemed to be running out of my head faster than my heart could pump it back up again. I tried to settle down. Mrs. Carter was reading something, but I didn't know what it was. I could hardly hear a thing in the room, except for my heartbeat.

"Are you feeling all right, Selwyn?" Mrs. Carter said.

"No, miss, I'm fine, I'm okay."

"Then why don't you read? It's your part."

"Yes, miss, I'll read it."

I felt the wave of pressure deep inside, and I felt the tigers creeping nearer, ready to pounce: I had to be ready. One wrong move and I'd be smashed. I could hear the roller now, swirling up in a gigantic arc beneath me, above me, through me. I tried to dive forward, to catch it at the perfect point, but I was upended. The wave came over me, tasting of salt and sea-sand and seaweed and bits of shell.

I watched the book go flying from my hands, and I remember seeing John Patel stretching his hand out toward me, trying to save my head from being crushed on the seabed, feeling his brown hand against my pale, white cheek, before I passed out.

Funnily enough, when I came around, I knew I'd been listening to music. I think it was jazz. A couple of electric guitars, a synthesizer, and a tenor saxophone weaving in and out of the main melody. I can't remember if there were drums, but I don't think so.

I was in the sickroom, and Mrs. Carter was there and some other woman I'd never seen before. Perhaps she was the school nurse. Neither of them was any use to me.

"Are you better, Selwyn?"

"Shouldn't we phone his mother?"

"Do you think he'd like some water?"

"No, a damp cloth on his head."

"Is he the South African boy?"

South African? South Africa? I could hear the words roaming around my head like they didn't have an owner.

South Africa? Is there such a place, or did I dream it up? Did I really kill Philemon Majodena? It couldn't have happened. Who would have thought that boy could have so much blood in him? It must have been a dream. A land of tigers. South Africa? With its beautiful purple mountains, the Drakensberg, the Dragon Mountains, lit up like cathedrals against the blue sky. Baboons laughing on the rocky crags, puff adders hiding in the dusty grass, waiting to put their venom in the first wrongly placed foot. Sunbirds, malachite sunbirds, gleaming metallic blue in the bushes. And rivers, clear as crystal glass, tumbling out of the kloofs, Mapopoman, Tugela. The Howick Falls. Plunging 140 meters over the cliff. And me, climbing down alone to the bottom of the falls. Dawn, before my folks woke up. From the bottom, looking up at the water plunging. Plunging straight out of the blue sky. Head spinning. What's the opposite of vertigo? Where you're in a place so deep and what you're looking at is so high that your head starts spinning. Was it a dream? Who could have dreamed up the Howick Falls? Who could ever have dreamed up South Africa? Who could have dreamed up Philemon Majodena lying in a pool of blood behind my old man's warehouse?

A dream that started in the Cape of Good Hope when I was born.

Images of my childhood passed through my consciousness with more reality than ever Bristol or England could attain, even if I lived a thousand years.

Cape Town, city of my birth. Table Mountain, with its white tablecloth of clouds, towering over me

33

for the first seven years of my life. The house looking up at the Devil's Peak, and beyond, in the distance, the Twelve Apostles, overlooking the same
Atlantic that beats on England's shores.

Ag, no, man, it's not possible! Let's begin again,
or end it once and for all.

"His mother's on the way."

"Well done."

"His color's coming back, don't you think?"

"Do you think so?"

Hiking with my old man. Being carried on his
back when I got tired, my arms holding him around
his neck. Khaki safari suits and thick boots. Ruck-
sacks and packed chicken lunches. Thick walking
sticks in case any snakes reared their ugly heads.
The colored man who wanted to guide us up the
mountain, but my old man said he could find his
own way up the mountain without having to pay
someone to tell him where to put his foot.

"Selly, what's happened?"

"He just passed out in English class."

"Ag, please, Selly, speak to me, man. It's Ma."

Ma. Taking me and Lynette to the beach at Muizenberg. Painting her watercolors on the easel, orange
marigolds, playing tennis in her white skirt, giving
me soft jelly when I was sick in bed with bronchitis,
crying when my old man made fun of her painting.
Ma. I'm okay, Ma. I think I'm okay, Ma.

"Selly, say something to me. It's Ma."

I'm saying something, Ma. Can't you hear me?

"Are you saying something, Selly?"

"Ja, Ma, I'm okay, Ma. Oupa died a long way from home, didn't he, Ma?"

"Ag, Selly, don't think about such things now. Our home is in England now. We must leave all our worries behind. You just get yourself better, okay?"

Chapter 3

My old man worked very hard to establish himself
in Bristol. If you think about it, it couldn't have
been easy for him. He didn't know anything about
trading in England when he arrived, and he had to
learn it all. Especially about English foods. They're
different from South African. When I wake up in the
morning, I still miss my Post Toasties, and there's
no Black Cat peanut butter or Liquifruit over here.
So my old man had to work hard. Often he left
home at seven in the morning and didn't return
until after ten at night. I suppose he wanted to make
a go of it, so that we could one day have the same

standard of living we had in South Africa. I didn't actually think it would ever happen, but still.

He worked helluva hard in Joburg to get the wholesale business moving. When he took it over, he was only supplying foodstuffs to Joburg, but at the time we left, he was supplying to the whole Rand, as far as Springs on the one side and Randfontein on the other.

We didn't get to see much of him in Bristol. And when we did, boy, was he grumpy. He's a moody man at the best of times, my old man, but jeez, when he gets tired, he's like the devil with a blister on his big toe.

My ma always hated it when he got like that. She used to say that he should get himself checked for diabetes because she read somewhere that diabetics get terrible moods when their blood sugar is all wrong. But he never got it checked 'cause it was her idea, not his.

She just had to make the best of it. It was difficult for her, too, because she had never worked in her life, and now she was trying to work in this real estate agency three days a week. Most of the rest of the time she had to do the cooking and cleaning. She was just like a servant, she moaned to my old man. It must have been a helluva change for her. She used to be queen of the ball, man. I mean, she just used to have lots of friends.

But in those months in Bristol, she must have been lonely. She wasn't her cheerful self like she used to be, always chatting to Stelly and me and phoning Lynette in Australia and telling her all the latest. No, she seemed to clam up a lot, and she often burst into tears when you didn't expect it. I felt sorry for her.

She was good at making friends, like I said before, but it's not that easy to make friends with English people. In South Africa, if you meet someone you like, you just say, "Hey, come over for a braai this Sunday!" *Braai* is short for *braaivleis,* and it means "a barbecue," a real South African barbecue with T-bone steaks and chops and boerewors—I really don't think there's an English word for this, but it translates as "farmers' sausages," and they're delicious!—and watermelon and Cokes, or beers for the adults. And even if you've only met that person for the first time, they'll turn up for the braai that Sunday, and then you're friends after that—easy, isn't it? But in England it's a different story. My ma says no one comes over for a meal until you've met them in the pub a few times. I don't know what they're nips of; maybe they'll catch each other's germs. I think maybe it's because this country's so damn freezing cold—nobody wants to go to someone else's house in case it's not as warm as their own place.

Ma didn't manage to get such a social life going here in Bristol, but probably that's because of her job taking three days of the week. The other two days of the week weren't full up with appointments and visits like in Joburg. She spent a lot of time doing her hair and putting on her makeup and her perfume, trying to capture her youth again. But not all the perfumes in Arabia could hide her worries.

She wasn't worried about Stelly. No, Stelly was okay. She was nicely settled at school and had made lots of friends. I thought it was me she was worried about. Until I found out later it wasn't. I thought she was worried that I wasn't making friends and that I wasn't settling down at school and that I wasn't getting over my oupa's passing away and that I had fainted at school. But later I knew it all worried me a lot more than it worried her.

There was a time when she worried about me. That was when the family moved to Joburg when I was seven. It was a year after Stelly was born and Lynette, I think, was in standard seven. The reason for the move was supposed to be my bronchitis, because Cape Town is at sea level, but Joburg is on the highveld—that's two thousand meters above sea level. Joburg was supposed to be good for bronchitis sufferers, and it was for me. It all cleared up. Not all the time I lived in Joburg did I ever get bronchitis. And yet in Cape Town, every second week I was seeing Dr. Weiss, getting my chest examined and my ears, nose, and throat poked about with little sticks and tools. And then for all my troubles, sometimes he used to give me a plaster of Paris model of Dopey or Snoozy or something. In the end I had the whole tribe of dwarfs.

But when we moved, I didn't settle in well at first in Joburg. So I suppose that was a ray of hope to keep me going. It took a year or so before I felt like I was one of the mob. And some of the friends I made then, when I was seven years old or so, like Joel and Gav, I kept until I left Joburg.

I think I'm just a slow settler. But really, between you and me and the lamppost, I think things were going from bad to worse for me in Bristol every day that passed.

They got a lot worse every time I skipped school, which was at least once a week, sometimes more. I thought the school must have told my parents, but no one had said anything to me yet. When I think back on it, I can't understand why no action was taken at that time. After all, I was asking for it, wasn't I?

I always went to the same place to sit, with a good view of the gorge in Clifton and the suspension bridge. Every time I was up there, I tried to feel the silence. Tried to listen out if another wave was on the way. I hadn't handled the last one too well at all.

By now, I'd learned that the bridge was a favorite spot for suicides, but I couldn't understand why. It was such a horrible, messy way to go. But I had noticed the Samaritans advertising on the bridge, presumably to give someone the idea of phoning them for help rather than jumping, although there was no telephone box nearby as far as I could see.

It was an enormous distance down into the gorge. That Brunel fellow had some nerve to build a bridge across that chasm. That's what I needed to do, desperately. Build a bridge across the chasm that had opened inside myself since the move to England, a chasm that was widening and deepening every day. I wondered who the Brunel was today who could bridge that sort of chasm for me. Not the Samaritans, anyway.

I read something about Brunel at that time. Apparently he built a tunnel at a place called Box—I don't know where that is, but he built it in such a way that once a year, on his birthday, the sun would shine directly through the center of the tunnel. The only thing he didn't take into consideration is that the sun can't be counted on to shine in this country more than a few days a year. Brunel would have had to engineer something sensational to shift the clouds on his birthday if he wanted that idea to work.

I'd come across that same idea before. You know where? At the Voortrekker Monument in Pretoria. That monument is a huge building, mostly hollow, with a tomb or something like that in the basement, and a tiny little hole somewhere in the roof. Once a year, on the Day of the Vow, the sunlight shines through onto that tomb. It's supposed to celebrate the time during the Great Trek, when the Voortrekkers made a vow with God that if he would give them a miraculous victory over the blacks at the battle the following day, they would remember that day forevermore. The Voortrekkers were badly outnumbered by the Zulus, but they had guns and the Zulus only had their short stabbing assegaais.

Well, you can guess. They must have won that battle because now there's that massive monument in Pretoria. And every year there's a public holiday, and thousands of Afrikaans South Africans go there to celebrate their superiority over the blacks. And the battle was called the Battle of Blood River because the river turned red with blood that day.

I've also been to that Voortrekker Monument, but only as a sort of tourist and not on the Day of the Vow. I climbed all the way to the top, and you get this incredible view of the surrounding area. It's very high, like a skyscraper, I suppose, even though it's shaped like a monument. I wasn't scared at the height so much when I was outside looking at the view. But there's one spooky part that made my stomach feel sick. And that was near the top inside. It's sort of curved like the top of an eggshell, and you walk up stairs over this curve, until you come to the highest point of the eggshell. Then there's a railing, and you can look over down to the floor below. You can even see the tomb in the basement from there, I think, but I may be wrong—it's a long time since I was last there.

The feeling of looking over the railing really scared me. Maybe I suffer from vertigo or something. You know why I was scared? Not because it wasn't safe or anything, but because there was a stupid voice in my very own head saying "Jump! Jump! Jump!" I never understood that. But it's the same thing I felt those days when I sat at the Clifton gorge. I heard this voice saying "Jump! Jump! Jump!" but it didn't mean jump off the edge of the cliff. No, it meant for me to jump off the cliffs inside myself. You know, this poet Gerard Manley Hopkins knew about those inside cliffs. He said the mind has got mountains with cliffs that are sheer, frightful, and no-man-fathomed. That's a spectacular word, hey, no-man-fathomed! I mean Clifton gorge is deep, but the cliffs inside are no-man-fathomed. Jeez, it scared me thinking about it. But still I went back there every week. I suppose it's the feeling parachutists get every time they're up in an airplane—the only diffs was I didn't have a parachute.

One time, after sitting at the gorge for a few hours, I went to my usual place in the antiques market to get a Coke and have a sit down where I could watch the trendies. I'm not a trendy at all, really, but I like watching trendies. They turn the world into a movie house, where you see the actors wearing different costumes every show.

But this one time I'm telling you about, it wasn't the trendies that made the world a movie house. No way! And I'll tell you something else; the movie that day was mad! It was one of those movies when you don't know what the hell's going on. Either they're not showing the whole thing (which often happens in South Africa because the government censors all the films—and all books too—that have anything to do with sex or communists), or the film is kak, that means real crap, and you don't know why anybody's doing anything.

This is what happened—I still can't believe it. I was just going into the antiques market when I look across the road and I see this posh red parked car, a Porsche or a Mercedes Sports or something. I'm not too good on cars. And then something caught my eye. I've already told you that I didn't ever think I was a racist, but seeing things I wasn't used to sent the shivers up my back. Anyway, I see this black guy putting his arm around this white chick and pulling her close to him for a kiss. Automatically, I did get that funny feeling, without asking for it at all. The couple look all lovey-dovey at each other—I'm seeing all this from behind, mind you, but I'm so fascinated I can't keep my eyes off it—and then they get out of the car. The bloke goes round to the woman's side, puts his arm around her, and leads her like that to this row of squashed-up houses. (I only call them squashed-up because they're not detached like in Joburg, but I bet they're expensive as hell.) He fiddles with his key ring for a minute and then opens the front door of his pad and lets her in. But just before he goes in, the woman looks around suspiciously to see that no one's watching. Man, you could tell that woman was having an affair with that bloke just by that one movement of hers.

But that's when the film goes completely bananas or else my head does. Because I recognize that woman. I've seen her before. Of course you have, you bladdy bedonnered donkey! It's your ma!

Shit, my head was spinning! "Play the film again!" I'm shouting to the projectionist, but the couple shut the door behind them and go up to do God knows what to each other.

After that, I didn't know if I was Arthur or Martha. I couldn't go and sit in that café while my ma was slogging it off with some black guy she hardly knew who was smart enough to own a Porsche. Why? Why? Why? Why?

Man, I knew my ma was a socializer, but not a bladdy slut.

I'm telling you, the ground could have opened under my feet and I could have fallen deep into the middle of the earth and still I wouldn't have been more shocked than at that moment. Actually, I think that's what happened. I fell and fell, just like that picture of Alice in Wonderland where she's falling and falling and falling, forever and ever, and she doesn't know who or what she'll be when she lands.

That fall was a long way. My old man fell down an elevator shaft in Roodepoort one Christmas. No, 'strues bob, man, I'm not making this up. He fell twenty-five meters down the elevator shaft!

He was at this party at one of the big food companies, in one of their offices, and when the party finished, he says good-bye to everyone. And he's not that drunk either—my old man at that time had never been a big drinker—but he was a little tipsy, thank goodness. Because that tipsiness, the doctor said, saved his life. It helped him relax while he was falling. Anyway, he says good-bye to the other people, walks to the elevator, presses the button—this is on the third floor, hey—and the doors open. He's still turning around saying good-bye to everyone and he walks into the elevator, just like anyone would, drunk or sober. Only one problem—no elevator! The bladdy machinery plays up, and the elevator is stuck at the bottom, ground floor.

Now you're not gonna believe this, but on my oath it's true because I saw the photo my dad took of that elevator the next day. The roof of the elevator that was waiting down below for him to fall on top of, that roof was made of solid iron—not only solid, but it had horrible points sticking up, the top of giant bolts and that sort of thing and some other jagged parts to do with the pulley. Now I'm still on oath, so this is true; the whole of that roof was solid metal except for a wooden trapdoor, the size of an ordinary trapdoor, about half a meter square or something. And guess where he fell. Right through the wooden trapdoor! Do you believe in miracles, man? That was one if I ever saw one.

The guests at that party saw my old man drop down that shaft, and they ran down the staircase to the ground floor to wipe up the mess. But when they get there, there's a living ghost walking out of the elevator, just as if he'd taken the elevator normally down those three stories. The only mark on him was between his eyebrows, and you know what that was from? Inside the elevator on the ground floor was a paraffin tin. And when my old man fell through that trapdoor, he hit his forehead on that tin. But that was the only mark. And his jacket was torn, just as if it had been cut by a rabbi at a funeral, just a few centimeters of rip, that's all. He walks out of that elevator and the guests are backing away from him. They think he's a ghost or something. And he says good-bye again and he's not hurt and climbs into his car and drives himself to the hospital. No internal injuries, nothing! What do you think of that?

Well, when I saw my ma whoring with that bloke, I thought, hell's bells, my old man was saved by that miracle for what reason? So he could go to England and have his wife cheat on him?

I tell you, the hole I fell into that night was deeper than that elevator shaft, and it didn't have a wooden trapdoor to break my fall. Flat onto the metal I fell, my whole world giving up all in one breath.

How could I ever look that woman in the eye again? What was I going to say to my old man? Hey, man, your wife's having it off with that black guy you met the other day. That's right, the black bloke who was with his wife. Definitely him—do you think I'd lie to you about something like that?

No way could I say that to him. It's not that easy to speak to your old man about things like that. I knew I would have to be dumb, like a witness to a murder who is struck with complete paralysis.

I couldn't go on living there anymore. The phoniness of it. It's bad enough living in this Coca-Cola stage set where phoniness is it. But to have it shoved in your nose every morning, noon, and night. No way.

Was that really my ma? The woman they had to cut me out of in that maternity home fifteen years ago? I couldn't believe it. I'm sure it would have been easier to believe it was a clone copy of her or something.

Before I got home, I was sick, vomiting in the gutter. And when I got home, I was sick again in the bathroom. And then I started another silence. I knew it would be a long one.

Chapter 4

The week after I saw my ma in Clifton was very bad for me. I couldn't talk to either of them. My ma was out a lot of the time anyway. I could just imagine where she was.

My old man wasn't around much either. He said it was a busy week, and most nights he didn't come home before ten.

When they were together, I didn't hear them arguing much, so I don't think my old man knew.

My ma had a lot of gall. What proved it was her inviting the black guy and his wife around for dinner one evening. I couldn't believe it. She got herself all dolled up and they talked and talked like old friends, even though they hadn't known each other more than a month and a half at the most.

The car parked outside was the same one I'd seen in Clifton. It wasn't a Porsche; it was a Mazda. There was no way I was going to stick around listening to them all being phony to each other, pretending to his wife and my old man that there was nothing more going on. Man, it was like a river of molten shit flowing under the very table they were eating at.

Ja, that was the pits for me. I just went upstairs to my bedroom and sat sulking like a castrated sheep. I didn't speak, I didn't come down for snacks—nothing! I just sat with my head in my hands. Not crying. Just sitting slowly, if you know what I mean.

They all went on chatting well into the night, and when I heard the Mazda drive off, I heard my old man come upstairs and say to Ma, "Nice people! They're really quite intelligent."

"Of course they are," my ma said. "He teaches at the polytechnic."

That beats me. My old man's calling him a nice guy, while the bloke himself is having the time of his life with my old man's woman—I mean Ma, of course—day after day.

The phoniness continued a few nights later when Ginny and Rosalie came over. I said I'd talk to Rosalie the next time I got a chance, but the way I was feeling, I wasn't in the mood for talking to anyone. I would have gone upstairs to my room and avoided the whole thing, but that would have caused an even greater commotion, seeing as Rosalie was only coming because I was the same age.

My ma was suddenly her old self again. She made conversation the whole night, like it was the end of the world and she better get in as much as possible before then. Ginny and Ma got on well together. My old man came home late, as usual, but he was polite to the two visitors. Before he came home, I heard Ma and Ginny having this conversation about how black men have got a lot of rhythm and how lithe their bodies are. It made me feel like puking, but I held it in. In all fairness, it was Ginny who started that conversation. Ginny is a divorcée, and she talks a lot about that sort of stuff. When my old man came home, I thought, okay, I've done my duty. I've stayed down till ten o'clock; that's enough. And I said I was going upstairs 'cause I had a headache. I hadn't talked to Rosalie like I said I would.

The next thing that happened amazed me. Rosalie got up too. Crikey Moses! She told her ma she was coming up with me and to call her when she was ready to go.

I was trapped.

I'd never had a girl in my bedroom, not even in Joburg. The reason is I was very shy of white girls. Did I say white? Ja, looking back, I can see that I was. I remember this time I went to a dance party at my friend Irwin's house. To warm things up, they played Spin the Bottle. You know the game. The boys take turns to spin the bottle. Whoever it points to, you have to kiss. Well, that was the first time I ever played that game—and the last. I was thirteen at the time.

Some other okes—I can't stop talking with these words; sorry, an oke is just a guy, you know, like a bloke—took their turns and made a big song and dance out of kissing these girls on the lips. Then suddenly it was my turn. I spun the bottle, truly hoping it would point to the sky or something, so that I wouldn't have to kiss anyone. But of course it didn't. It landed pointing straight at this girl Kerren. Now Kerren's okay; she's pretty and all that, and she's young, actually the sister of an oke in my class called Maxie. She was ready for the kiss, all right, but I froze. I tell you, it's cold in England and sometimes you freeze. But the way I froze that night, I felt like it was my brain. Nothing moved. I couldn't go forward to kiss her, and I couldn't go backward to get away.

"Selly's poep-scared," Nobby said.

"Sistog, man, he's a pipsqueak," Maxie said. "Kerren won't bite."

"Just give her the kiss, man, and let's get on with it," another oke said. "It's my turn next."

"I'll kiss her for you," Joel said.

Suddenly there was a millimeter of movement in my brain—one millimeter of thought.

I kissed my own fingers and planted it on her lips.

"That doesn't count, domkop! Give her a proper kiss." A domkop is a dumbhead.

"It has to be on her properly. You can't send it in a telegram."

"Why are we waiting?"

51

They started a slow hand clapping.

All this time Kerren stood near me, waiting for her kiss. I wanted to tell her, it's not because you're ugly or anything. 'Strues God, it's not. It's because you're pretty. I wanted to tell her that, but the freeze didn't let up, and anyway, I couldn't have said anything like that in front of the other okes.

"One more minute, Selly, and then we're going to push your lips onto Kerren's lips and make them kiss together."

I looked at Kerren. She was lekker. And she took pity on me, thank goodness. She lifted her hand to my lips so that I could kiss that instead.

I took her hand carefully and kissed the very tip of the pinky finger—only the very tip. That's how shy I was.

And I never played Spin the Bottle again.

And now there was a girl coming up to my room. Another lekker-looking girl. Oh jeez, help, man!

"That was a good idea of yours to say you had a headache," Rosalie said.

Hey, it *was* a good idea. But she wasn't meant to follow me up.

"I was fed up with their conversation," she said.

I didn't know where to put myself in my own room. I didn't want to go near my own bed, and I thought I better leave the chair for her. So I sort of leaned up against the window.

"You don't talk much," she said.

I didn't answer.

"Do you like it in England?" she asked.

I shook my head to mean no, I don't like it.

"I had a bad time also, at first," she said. "My parents got divorced in the first year they were here."

She told me all about it. By the sound of it, I thought her old man must have been a communist in South Africa. The South African government calls anyone a communist who stirs up trouble to help black people, and that's what he sounded like to me. He got put in jail in Johannesburg and was in solitary confinement for months and months and months. And then he got deported to England. And his wife, Ginny, joined him here, but he kept on with his anti-apartheid stuff, and she wanted a new life without so much politics and couldn't stand it anymore, so they got divorced.

"But I still see my dad a lot. He lives in Dorking. I go there for weekends."

Then she looked at me like nobody has ever looked at me before. Don't get me wrong. I don't mean she was flirting or anything. But she looked at me like she was trying to fit a puzzle together. Like there were pieces missing, and she couldn't find them.

"Why don't you ever talk to me?"

I didn't answer.

"Don't you like me?"

Still no answer from my mouth. But I let my head nod up and down just a centimeter or two.

"Are you shy?"

Again I nodded a centimeter or two.

"Every time I've come here, you seem to look at me as if you like me. And at your oupa's funeral you kept staring at me. I thought you must like me a little bit."

She took a step forward from where she was standing by my desk, so that she was very near to me. Then she put her arm around my shoulder, but I panicked and pulled away. That sort of closeness could lead in a million directions, and I was scared of them all.

She took a step backward.

"I'm sorry. I didn't mean it badly. You can talk to me if you want. It's all right," she said.

I think I would have paid a million rands at that moment to make my voice say something (if I had a million rands). I don't know what I would have liked to say. But anything would have done, just to break the ice. But the ice was thick, man, and it was all in my head, not in hers and not between us. It was right in my own head.

She stepped back to the desk and saw my Sylvia Plath book lying on my pad on the desk.

"Do you read poetry?"

I nodded.

"I like it also," she said. "Sylvia Plath was an exile, just like us. Homesick, she was. It's terrible that she killed herself, hey, isn't it?"

She put the Sylvia Plath down again, but in a different place from where it was before. Now the pad was there where she could see it. It had one of my poems on it.

"You write also?" she said, picking up the pad. "Do you mind if I read it?"

It was a poem about a bell jar. No air inside to breathe. Just a person sitting slowly in it. Looking around. And there's a wind blowing tiny scraps of newspaper around the jar. With pictures of Oupa and Ouma Fanny and whores with their arms around their blokes and a dead black boy with his pants held around his stomach with a piece of string and blood on his shirt.

I jumped forward and snatched the pad from her hand.

"Sorry!" she said. "Sorry! I shouldn't have touched it."

She really looked sorry, too. If only I could have told her, don't be sorry, it's not your fault, it's me. I'm screwed up and I don't want you to see how screwed up I am.

"Sorry! But I'd love to read your poems. I'll never ask you again. But if you ever want to show me one, I'd love to read it. It would mean a lot to me."

"Rosalie! Rosalie! We're going now. Come on now, don't dawdle!"

Rosalie ignored her mother's voice calling.

"Listen, Selwyn. You're okay."

And then she was gone.

And I was left standing in my bell jar, with no air, and a scrap of newspaper flying around with this lekker girl's face and body on it, and the name of the girl was Rosalie, and she even liked poetry, same as me, and I couldn't breathe 'cause there was no air. Why didn't I talk to her? I must have been crazy not to talk to her. Crazy as hell. Why did I pull away from her? She was being nice. She would never come around again; she would never speak to me again. I must have been mad. Mad as hell.

And I was falling through that elevator shaft down into the center of the earth, deeper than I ever fell before.

And the wave was a huge mountain of a wave, rolling down on me with the sound of a thunder-blast.

And I was in a dead end. With all my own problems standing there with knives. A whole gang of tsotsis, and I tell you, tsotsis are black thugs. Except they don't have to be black—any gangster is a tsotsi. And these tsotsis surrounded me, and they were coming for me. And if they didn't get me that night, it would be another time; I knew it.

I felt the knife in my stomach. One of them must have stabbed me while I wasn't noticing. And the blade went deep and the blood ran out. And when they came to find me, I'd look like Philemon Majodena, lying in a pool of blood.

Chapter 5

The next few days were bad. I didn't speak to anyone. I just kept silent. For three days.

I only went to school once and skipped the rest.

I spent a lot of time at the gorge, staring down into the chasm.

I thought a lot about my old man. He was beginning to look old and stooped. He's forty-four, and I tell you, he looked as old as that. His hair was thinning out and his moustache was starting to go grey all over and his eyes looked always tired. Maybe it was from working so hard, but maybe he was beginning to have his suspicions about my ma.

She was out of the house more and more, running

around with her black playboy, probably. And she and my old man hardly ever spoke. And I think his work started to go badly at that time. Maybe from all the worry. I thought maybe he was even more worried about me. I didn't know—he never said a word to me about anything. He wasn't the sort who ever talked about his problems.

One day I came home from the gorge, and my old man's car was outside the house.

Jeez, that's unusual, I thought. He never came home before ten at night, and it was only five in the afternoon.

I walked around the house. No sign of anyone. Ma was out as usual. I knew where she was! Socializing!

Then I heard a sort of cry from upstairs. Maybe my old man was sick, I thought. I went up to his bedroom and pushed open the door.

He was there, all right. He was sitting on the side of the bed with his elbows on his knees and his bony fingers covering his face. Folded up like that, his tall body looked so defeated and pitiful. He didn't even hear me come in.

And you know what he was doing? Crying, man. Like a little baby. Howling. And sniveling in between the howls. It was pathetic. I'd never, ever seen him cry before, not in my whole life. Man, that guy was really crying his heart out. I don't think I ever saw anyone cry like that. It was as if I could see a mine dump of worry sitting on his shoulders, crushing him, breaking him, breaking his person into bits of nothing.

I couldn't move. I wanted to leave him to his own grief, but I couldn't move from the spot. Part of me just wanted to see the suffering.

Hell, I used to love my old man. I don't think anyone ever loved his dad the way I did. Until I was twelve and he bought the revolver. Then I got scared of him. And I could see he was a scared person, too.

But before he bought that gun, boy, did I love him. I thought he was the greatest dad a guy could have. I used to call him my best friend. I even told my friends that my old man was my best friend. We used to do everything together. We used to play rugby, just the two of us in our garden. We had seven-eighths of an acre, and most of it was in the back of the house. We used to play by the side of the three palm trees, him on one side and me on the other. Gaining ground we used to play or left-foot kicking or dropkicks only or points for catching cleanly. Sometimes the ball used to land in the middle of these fat palm trees. Then we had to get a ladder, and my old man would climb up and try to get the ball out with a long pole. But there were huge palm thorns at the bottom of the leaves. They were longer and thicker than knitting needles, with this hard, hard point, and they were sharp, man, and if they stuck you, then you'd really know about it. I don't know if they had poison on the tip or what, but it was a bad business if you got speared by one of them. Sometimes the ball got speared—right through the leather. Then we'd have a laugh and play cricket for a few days until it was repaired or he bought another rugby ball. Sometimes we'd play rugby until it was so dark you couldn't see the ball and my ma was calling us for supper and the supper was getting cold, but we had to finish our game, especially if my old man was losing, 'cause he was a bad sport. But I didn't mind him being a bad sport, 'cause I was, too. It just made the game more competitive.

And the best moment of all was once my old man and my oupa came to watch me play rugby for my school against Jeppe Boys. It was a helluva hard game 'cause Jeppe were good. And my old man and my oupa were standing on the sideline watching the game. And there was a scrum right near the opposition line, just near where they were standing. And we won the scrum. And the ball came around the blind side and was passed to me. I dodged two boys in the black Jeppe stripes and dived over for a try in the corner, right under my old man's nose, almost.

But it wasn't only rugby. We also used to play billiards and snooker. We had this table we bought so that Oupa could enjoy himself when he came to stay with us for holidays. He loved billiards, even though his hands weren't too steady. If he missed the ball he was aiming at, he'd take the white ball back and make a big pretense of cleaning a spot of dirt off the table. We never scored foul shots against him.

But the games with my old man were different. That was more serious. All foul shots counted. And we played for money most times. Not a lot of money. But it was exciting. My old man was better than me, but sometimes I used to win, and sometimes he used to let me win my money back, double or quits.

He really was great fun. We used to go swimming at my parents' country club. Sometimes we used to go in big groups with my parents' friends, but mostly it was just our family. My old man and me used to get in the water as soon as we got there, and we didn't get out until they chucked us out when the sun was setting. We used to have all sorts of competitions: Who could swim farthest underwater? Who was fastest over one length or two? (Neither of us was any good at long-distance swimming.) Who could do the best somersault dive? Who could do the best bomb dive? Who could walk farthest on his hands with his legs sticking out of the water?

The only thing that wasn't perfect about my old man was his moods. Like I told you before, when he was cross, he was like the devil with a blister on his big toe. But when I turned twelve and he bought the revolver—that's when I got worried about his moods. I used to think that one day he might have a go at my ma or at me with that thing. I'll tell you why he bought it, though. It's because we lived on seven-eighths of an acre. And if we would have been burgled or attacked, there was no way any neighbors would have heard us.

Anyway, since the recent spate of bombings, everyone we knew had built walls and bought guns. My old man also took some precautions. There were already burglar bars on all the windows of the house, every single one. Even my window that looked out on the Lady of Spain and the pond and the palm trees and the jacarandas. I always had to look out at those things through the burglar bars. They were quite good at protecting the house, though one time we were burgled when we were out. You know how? These black guys had a fishing rod with a string and razor blades all the way down the string and a fishing hook at the end of it. And they put the rod in through the bars of the window in my parents' room, and they fished out my ma's necklace. But it wasn't a good necklace anyway. You know how I know about the fishing rod with the razor blades? Because they dropped it in the street outside our house. I think some dog must have chased them or something. Not our dog, though. Sweetie was locked inside the house while we were away.

Sweetie was an Alsatian, a huge one, but not one hundred percent pure. I'd say about ninety-nine point nine percent Alsatian. You know what gave it away? Her ears didn't stand up, that's all. She was a fantastic watchdog, with a heck of a loud bark. She barked at anyone who came through our front gates. But it was their own fault for coming in because we had a big sign on the gate which said BEWARE OF THE DOG! PASOP VIR DIE HOND!

Sweetie only ever bit black people. Don't get me wrong; she wasn't trained as a racist dog or anything. Like I said before, in our family we thought of ourselves as being against apartheid. We just took it for granted that Sweetie knew who was probably coming to steal and who wasn't. The only problem was Matilda's friends. When they came to visit her, they had a tough time getting past Sweetie. Sometimes we used to say "Ssssssaaaaa" to Sweetie, and it made her go mad. Her hair stood up on her back like she'd seen a ghost, and then she'd go charging off down the drive under the jacarandas, barking all the way. Most black people just backed off or stood at the fence and called, "Matil-da! Matil-da!" until Matilda came to give protection down the drive and all the way to her room at the back.

I think Sweetie only ever hurt one person. It was a black man selling something. He managed to walk all the way down the drive before Sweetie caught sight of him. He was selling something like compost 'cause he was carrying this heavy bag, and Sweetie bit the bag open, and the stuff poured out, and the man ran all the way down the drive with Sweetie chasing and barking and the stuff pouring out of his bag. And at the end of the drive, when he'd lost all the contents of the bag, he made the mistake of turning around and swearing at Sweetie, and she bit him out there in the street.

But I was telling you about the revolver. My old man decided the burglar bars and Sweetie weren't enough protection, so he also put up a big wrought iron door on the outside of our front door. And afterward we used to call that the Colditz door. And he had this six-foot wall built around the property, with spikes along the top of it. And he also bought the revolver and bullets.

He kept that revolver in its leather holster next to his bed at night and locked it in a cupboard during the day, so that Matilda wouldn't see it.

I didn't like the look of that revolver. It had power. Killing power. But it also meant we were vulnerable. If my old man needed a revolver, then it must mean he was scared. That was the first time I ever thought my old man was scared of anything.

It was a long journey from the day he bought that revolver to seeing him crying his heart out on that bed. Next to his bed there was a bottle of whisky, half drunk, and a glass tipped on its side.

I was paralyzed by seeing him like that. My eyes were alive but nothing else.

Then my thoughts started moving again. I backed out of the room silently, then pretended to open the door quite noisily and stepped into the room again.

My old man looked up. His bloodshot eyes were filled with loathing and self-pity.

"Voetsek, man!" he shouted at me. That's the word for shouting at an animal or someone you despise. He'd never used that word on me before.

"Ag, Monty, what's wrong, man?"

I've always called my old man by his first name ever since I can remember. Those were the first words that passed my lips in three days.

"Voetsek!" he shouted. "Leave me alone!"

"Monty, have I done something wrong to you?"

"You're all wrong, man. You're growing up just like me. A loser."

"Are you a loser, Monty?"

"I've lost everything," he said, shaking his head and waving me out of the room as he started howling again.

I wanted to go up to him and say, "Come on,

Monty, let's go outside and have a game of rugby" or "Come on, Monty, let's go for a swim" or just plain simply, "Come on, Monty, cheer up, she still loves you, man, and I'll make friends here in this godforsaken place, and your work will be okay; we'll get rich." But I couldn't bring myself to say lies and I left him there and I knew he wasn't worried about me at all because actually he hated me, he hated me, he hated me for everything that had happened, not just in Bristol but at the warehouse, too, and my ma didn't care either. I saw it clearly—she didn't care about my old man anymore and she didn't care about me; all she cared about was pretending she was a liberated woman who could mess around with black playboys, and I was in a dead end, and that meant an end where death was waiting, waiting, that door with the footsteps behind, and I wanted to knock on that door and say, "Make me forget! Please, man, make me forget South Africa and Philemon Majodena and my ma and her black playboy and my old man who's a loser, and me, the biggest loser of them all," and my mind was crawling with scorpions and I went upstairs to the bathroom and got the bottle of aspirin and another bottle of paracetamol and a box of antihistamines just for good luck, and I also got a glass of water and a plastic mug, too, and I took them all to my room, and I tipped the bottles out onto my desk and ripped the antihistamines from their sealed sheets and made a pile of tablets, and my old man told me to voetsek and I would; I would voetsek right out of his life and out of my ma's life.

I didn't know how deep that elevator shaft went into the center of the earth, but it was time to find out. But first things first. I tore up all the poems I had written, every single one, into tiny little pieces no bigger than a one-cent coin. I made a pile of them, too. Then I threw them into the air and scattered them all over my room, so that they were flying around my bell jar, the scattered pieces of my life, and no one would ever make sense of them, and even the gold ink the poems were written with seemed to be phony, and I could hear those man-eaters approaching, hear the footsteps behind death's door getting really close, and I wondered if I ever got inside there, would I still be so shy, and would they cross-question me about Philemon Majodena because no one had ever asked me anything about him on this earth, and would I ever be forgiven?

I swallowed the tablets in handfuls, half choking myself in the process, and I kept swallowing until I felt sick, and I didn't want to vomit, so I stopped taking any more, and I lay down on the bed and read the poem in a book that I opened on my bed, and it was by Keats. I used to like this poem so much. It's the one about fading away and dissolving and forgetting the weariness of all the people in the world, who are sick of life and groaning, and going to join the nightingale, but I've never seen a nightingale and I've never heard one either, but I just think of that place where they make the gold ink and I want them to put me into that hot furnace so that I melted and became pure gold ink, and I wanted to be like this film I once saw of Francis of Assisi, where he threw away his phoniness, took off his rich clothes, and stood naked in a public square, just himself with his liquid gold blood, and I lay naked on my bed with just a white towel over my private parts, and I faded away, falling through story after story, through the elevator on the ground floor, deep into the earth where my oupa was buried, deeper still, and someone was sucking out the air in the bell jar, and my life was like a brief candle giving its last flicker, and the ultimate wave was breaking on a beach, the last wave of all, I was the last of the surf riders, and I missed the wave and it threw me into a place where there was no sea, no air, no elevator shafts, no bell jars, no gold ink

Chapter 6

There was this book I heard about once, a history of South Africa, and it was published in England, and they wanted to bring out a version of it to sell in South Africa. But the censors didn't agree with one of the chapters, the one that let black South African leaders speak for themselves. The government was afraid of giving those people a voice, so you know what they did? (I never saw the book, I must admit, but I heard about it from someone who probably knew what he was talking about.) I'll tell you what they did. The version to be sold in South Africa was printed with forty blank pages—absolutely blank. Not a single word on any of them. (Maybe it had the page number, but I'm not sure.)

My family used to joke about those pages. We used to say it was blank for each person to write their own version of history.

Anyway, what I'm trying to do is to explain to you why the previous two pages of this book were blank. It's because I don't have a version of what happened to tell you. After I swallowed the tablets, everything was blank. I was in a total dwaal, wandering through the mountains of my mind, confused and with no road signs. You can write your own version of what happened to me if you like because I don't remember a thing.

When I came around, I was in the hospital. I don't want to say much about that. They pumped my stomach, and apparently what saved my life was that feeling that I was going to vomit because I stopped taking more tablets, and what I had already swallowed wasn't enough to kill me.

I spent three days in the hospital until they knew my stomach was okay.

My ma and my old man came to visit me, and they put on a good show. Anyone watching us would have thought we were a regular family and that I was in there just having my appendix out. My ma looked like she was concerned about me, and one or two tears even dropped from her eyes, which she had to wipe with a tissue.

"Don't ever do anything like that again, Selly," she said. "You frightened us."

She held my dad's hand, and she tried to keep talking about lots of things, but not about black playboys or anything real.

And my old man pretended everything was okay again. He didn't even mention the time I saw him crying or his work or if he knew that his wife was two-timing him, and when he leaned over me once in bed, I thought I could smell whisky, and I felt like saying, "Come on, Monty, let's forget the pretending bullshit," but I didn't say it.

Stelly came in for a few minutes, and she hugged me and sat on the hospital bed.

"Hi, Selly, you look sick," she said. "When will you come home?"

Stelly was okay, you know. I used to tease her like mad in Joburg, but not as bad as the cat. That cat came from next door, and one day I got mad with it. I took it to the one room we had upstairs, and I locked it in and I put boxes and books all around the divan bed and shoved it underneath. And the cat was terrified, man. It tried to scratch its way out of there, but it was well and truly trapped in. And I jumped on the divan, up and down, making a tremendous racket, banging on it, and the cat was nearly out of its mind with terror. And it made this unearthly noise. I've never heard anything like it. Actually, I didn't know a small cat like that could make such a big sound—I mean, a sound like a grown man's voice, a moaning voice. I really terrified that cat, and I don't know why I did it. I was twelve then, and I only did it once. Usually I like animals like dogs and cats, but I frightened the shit out of that cat.

I never teased Stelly as badly as that, but I did give her a rough time when we lived in Joburg. Most of that stopped when we came to Bristol. I don't know why. But in Joburg I tormented her, that's what I did, usually until she cried. Then Lynette or someone would butt in, and I would be really nice to her again. Lynette always took her side and liked to make a fuss every now and again. But I was the one who played with Stelly the most. Lynette was too busy with boys most of the time.

She was boy mad. Lynette used to have really wild parties in our house, and the boys used to get drunk and have midnight swims in the pool. I had to be in bed early on those nights, but me and Stelly used to sneak to the kitchen window and spy on all the goings-on. Lynette didn't have my trouble with kissing, that's for sure. There was no kissing of pinky fingers with her. It was all lips and smooches and the whole works.

Stelly idolized me in some way, I think. I didn't deserve it, but I was her big brother, who looked after her when I wasn't tormenting her.

"I don't know when I'm coming home, Stelly," I said. "Maybe when I'm better."

There was a box of chocolates from Ginny and Rosalie with a get-well card that had a picture of flowers on it.

And a parcel from my school class. I opened it up. Inside there was a huge card with a stupid joke and everyone had signed their names, and some had put a few wisecracks and messages. I tell you, I didn't even recognize half the names, and I couldn't read some of them, and the wisecracks weren't wise at all, and the messages were phony like "Get well soon. The soccer team needs you'—that was from Mr. Wilson—and "Come back soon. School's not that bad!" signed *Jeff*, and "Hope you're better soon. Your mate Milton." That was a joke in itself, I thought, because he'd never been my mate. As well as the card, there was also a little battery-operated electronic game. You had to press buttons on it to make this little fat man hop across eight worlds to rescue a princess. I played with it for a bit, but I was useless at crossing even one world, never mind the other seven. I put it away in the drawer next to the bed.

I bet Gav and Nobby and Joel would have sent me good messages if they had known I was in the hospital. They would have said things that would have really made me laugh and cheered me up, like they really missed me. But they were six thousand miles away.

After the second day, I wanted to get out of that place. It was depressing.

Lying in that bed was like once when I went to sleep over at the home of this friend of mine called Bernard Morgenstern. I was eleven, and it was the first time I ever spent the night at his house.

Everything was okay until bedtime. He was lying in his bed on one side of the room, and I was on the other side in this bed that felt lumpy.

"Should we tell each other ghost stories?" he said.

"No, I don't like any," I said.

"What about skrikking each other?" A skrik is when you get a fright. "You tell me something bad, and then I'll tell you something bad."

"Come off it, man. I don't want to."

"Okay," he said. "Did you know that we got burgled last week?"

"No."

"Ja, I woke up and there was this African. I shot him with my catapult. The stone hit him in the head."

"Was he in your house?"

"Ja, just down the passage there."

"Weren't you frightened?"

"Ja, but he was coming down the passage, so I had to do something."

"And then what happened?"

"Nothing. He knocked me unconscious with his fist, so I don't remember anything else."

"So what happened to the burglar?"

"My old man got his gun, and the burglar ran off."

"Is it true?" I asked. "Or are you making it up?"

"On my mother's life, it's true. You can ask her tomorrow."

Later Bernard fell asleep, and I was left awake. And I wasn't frightened about the burglar, but I couldn't sleep. And then I got a stomachache and a headache, and I called Bernard's mother and I said I'm sick, and she said what do you want to do, should she call a doctor, and I said no, but I think she should take me home. And she did. At eleven o'clock at night. And when I got home, I vomited in the toilet, and my ma said I didn't have to go to school the next day. And I didn't. And I never slept over at his place again.

That's how I felt in that hospital. I wanted to go home, but home like it was in Joburg when I was eleven, before the trouble began. I didn't want to go to that Bristol terraced house that wasn't really home.

I wanted to go somewhere where I could sit slowly, where I could figure out why I was still alive and what I should do now. In Joburg the place I used to go to sit was the bird sanctuary. That was a nature reserve with a lake that had millions of reeds and bulrushes, and in those reeds were bishop birds. Now those birds were bright, not like the faded things you see in England. The birds in this country have no color. All the rain has washed out the colors, and there's no sun to make the birds shine. If you could see a bishop bird you would know what I mean. A bishop bird is bright, bright, bright, bright red. With a bit of black. Sometimes you could see a hundred bishop birds sitting on those reeds—sometimes even more.

That was a good place for sitting. It was near my house, and I could just walk there. And I used to sit slowly there and watch the bishop birds and also the herons, but they were on the other side of the lake. I liked to go there by myself, but I took Oupa there when he came for holidays, and he also knew it was a special place where a person could think.

A person needs a good place to sit slowly and think, like that bird sanctuary, but in Bristol in the beginning I didn't have one.

Actually, that sanctuary was nearly spoiled for me one time. I almost forgot to mention it. And you know who nearly spoiled it for me? The South African police. This is how they did that.

One time I was going there alone, and I passed this African man, who was walking by the gates of the sanctuary. He was well dressed for an African, I mean with a briefcase and smart jacket and tie on, and a walking stick. He just seemed to be walking there in the car park of the sanctuary.

Suddenly this police car turned up out of the blue. The African man didn't budge. He didn't try to make a run for it or anything. He didn't even look suspicious. Anyway, these two big policemen get out of the car and they go up to him. And he still looks innocent. They take his briefcase and they open it. He must have been a salesman or something, but I couldn't see what he was selling too clearly.

"Where do you live?" they ask him. "Do you have permission to live there? Where are your papers?"

They were pestering him like mad because Africans must have permission to live in their accommodation.

"It's here in my jacket, baas."

He fumbles around in his inside jacket pocket.

"Kom, kaffir, we haven't got till Christmas!" I've never liked saying that word he used because it's a bad swearword to use about black people. They hate it if you use it. But it's what the policeman said, so I'm telling you.

"It's here, baas, I had it this morning."

"Jy lieg, kaffir." That means "You're lying, black man." And both those policeman had revolvers strapped to them in shiny brown holsters.

"Ag, no, baas; it must be in my other jacket."

"What other jacket, man? You haven't got another jacket."

"Yes, I've got plenty jackets."

"A rich kaffir, hey?"

And I didn't hear the rest, but I think the police must have thought he was cheeky or something because next minute they were climbing all over him. They had him on the ground, and they were pulling his jacket and hitting him with his own walking stick, and their feet were kicking into his face. Then they grabbed his briefcase, pushed him into the car, and drove off at high speed. It made my blood boil to see people being so vicious, but there wasn't much I could do about it. That was what South African police were like, and I was terrified of them.

After that, it was difficult to go back to the sanctuary. But luckily for me, it all happened in the car park and not near the lake, so I said to myself, you don't sit in the car park, man, you sit by the lake. So I went back there one day, and it was okay. The bishop birds were still the same, and I could sit there without having too many memories of what happened in the car park.

Anyway, they kept me in the hospital in Bristol,

not because I was sick anymore, but because they didn't know what to do with me or where to send me either.

A psychiatrist asked me a lot of questions, but I thought they were stupid questions and I didn't answer them properly. But the thing that bothered him the most was where was I going to go after that hospital? I didn't know myself where I wanted to go. Until I could sit slowly somewhere and let my thoughts sort themselves out, I didn't know what I wanted. So I said I wasn't sure about going home. I think that psychiatrist was worried that my home situation had a lot to do with my being in the hospital at that moment. And I thought he was right, so I said I didn't want to go home.

That obviously pained my ma and my old man because they each looked at me in an odd way, as if to say, "Don't you love me anymore?" Jeez, I could have asked them the same question, no problem.

One surprising thing happened on the third day I was in that hospital. The ward sister came to me and said there was a girl asking to visit me and was it okay to let her in. She said the girl's name was Rosalie Morris. Rosalie? What was she doing there?

"Well, should I let her come in or not?"

I didn't know. Maybe it would start all the nonsense happening to me again; but then this was a hospital, and maybe they could help me if it did.

"Ja, okay," I said.

Rosalie looked good. She apologized for the card with the flowers.

"My mom chose it," she said.

"It's okay," I said.

The ice was broken. I couldn't believe it. I didn't have to pay millions of rands for the words to come out of my mouth. They just came without asking.

"I brought you something," she said, giving me a parcel wrapped with colorful paper.

I opened it. It was a special pad with a blue-patterned cover and a shiny pen with a dozen cartridges.

"Thanks a helluva lot," I said, and I meant it.

"I thought you might want to write some poems," she said.

"I don't know," I said. "I tore up all my others."

"Ag, shame," she said. "But now you can start again."

"Where's your ma?" I said.

"No, I came on my own."

"It was nice of you, thanks."

We spoke about a few other things, about films and what music we liked and about schools and what she wanted to do when she left school, and then she said she'd go, but she also said she'd come visit again if I stayed in that hospital.

"I don't know how long I'll stay here," I said. "I want to get out of here. It's damn depressing."

"It looks like it," she said. "Are you going to go home?"

"I don't know. I think I'll go crazy again if I go there."

"No, don't go crazy," she said. "The rest of the world's crazy enough without you joining them."

She looked at me and smiled, and I tell you, her smile really cheered me up.

"Yes, well, I'll see you," she said.

And she was gone.

I smelled the pad she had given me. It smelled nice, like new books do, and a bit leathery. And I held the new pen in my hand. I didn't feel like writing any poems, not in that hospital smelling of Jik or some detergent, but I felt like I would someday like to write poems with that pen. It had a good feel.

Chapter 7

In the end, they decided to send me to an adolescent unit. I came to this place, where I am now, that everyone calls the Villa. At that time, there were six other mixed-up kids like myself living there. Two of them had also attempted suicide, and one of those two had done it three times before. Jeez, he must have been bad at it or else he just wanted attention.

Actually, I got on fairly well with all the others, even though Kevin had this scrap with me. The one exception was Susan, but I must say I wasn't the only one who didn't get on with her. She was a real misery and tried her best to bring everyone down.

I couldn't understand with her way of looking at things, why she didn't try suicide herself. She thought that everyone was trying to get at her all the time, and she even accused me one day of being part of a conspiracy to get her out of the Villa. But I tell you I never conspired with nobody, not about Susan, not about anything.

But the others were okay. Especially one boy called Bradley, who was a West Indian. He was really into rap music and spent all of his day with earphones on, his hands and feet beating out rhythms nonstop.

The young black kids in South Africa can jive fantastically to the township music. The only time Matilda's boy came to see her, when she worked for us, I remember seeing this piccanin dancing in our backyard to the radio. He was only five, man. All of the rest of the time he lived four hundred miles away with his granny back in the homeland or somewhere, and we used to let Matilda go visit him once a year for a week at a time. But then one year she came back two days late, and my old man nearly chucked her out.

"Why you back late, Matilda? I nearly gave your job to someone else. There's plenty of girls who want this work, you know. Don't you want to keep your job?"

"No, master, don't give my job to the other girl. Please, baas."

"So why you come back late, then?"

"Ja, master, I got stabbed."

"Where did you get stabbed?"

"By my mother's gate, master."

"No, man, I mean where on your body? The wound couldn't have closed up already."

"Ja, master, it's on my leg."

"I can't see a stab wound on your leg. Was it a thorn stabbed you?"

"No, master, it was a long knife."

"So where's the stab, then?"

"Master, it's here," she said, and she lifted her skirt to show a white bandage around her thigh, turning her face away from us all as she did so.

"You sure that's a stab and not just a bandage?" my old man said.

"It's a stab, master. It's very deep. They took me to the hospital, and they sewed it with needle and cotton."

"All right, Matilda, this one time. Next time I give your job to the other girl."

"Yes, master. Thank you, baas."

"And don't bladdy mess around with people who carry knives."

"No, master."

I don't know what Matilda's boy was called, but he was a good jiver. My mother liked that boy and called him up on the back porch and gave him a cardboard box full of old clothes. I don't know if they were my clothes or Stelly's or whose. But that boy never came to stay again, and then Matilda left because she had heart trouble or something, and then we got another servant girl.

When Bradley wasn't listening to rap, you could have a good conversation with him. Not just about rap. He was a deep thinker, Bradley was. He understood a lot. His father used to beat him up horribly when he was a kid and still did, I think. But in spite of that, he didn't hate his father. In his shoes, I think I would have.

In the groups he was always the first to catch on when I spoke about something that happened in South Africa. He really understood me. And you know, I never had any trouble understanding him. Come to think of it, nobody in the Villa has ever had any trouble understanding my accent. Maybe they were just used to hearing crazy people talking, but I don't think so. I think they were good listeners because of the groups.

Sometimes Bradley's words were like rapping, and he could make good rhymes, like "Come, people; come, people; come to the Villa, but don't forget to bring pain-killer." The only trouble was that out of the blue Bradley ran off one day and never showed up again. I really missed him.

Now I want to tell you one thing that Bradley said. You know what it was? One day he was telling the group about his father. And he had this cushion in front of him, and the idea was to take out your feelings on the cushion if you wanted to, and he got really worked up this one time, and I thought definitely he was going to crack up, and Bala—that's our therapist—said, "Yes, Brad, hit that cushion! Hit it! It's your father. What would you like to say to your father about beating your head in?"

And suddenly, Bradley turned around and he went all calm and quiet and he looked around at us and then back at the cushion, and he spoke to the cushion very quietly and he said, "You're on the run. You've been on the run all your life. And now you're beating my head in so that I will start running. And then I'll be on the run as well. All my life."

"That's great, Brad; you've done well," Bala said.

"Great shit," Bradley said. "This cushion shit's a load of crap. You can shove your cushions where they belong. I'm not talking to no cushions."

And Bradley walked out of the group room, and nobody saw much of him that night. And by the next day, he was gone, and I never saw him again. Funny thing, though, he left everything behind. He didn't even pack a suitcase or anything—he just split. He even left his Walkman behind and his earphones and his tapes. I couldn't figure it out.

But what he said about his old man being on the run really stuck with me. On the run. That describes my old man so accurately. I really saw it for the first time.

I never hit that cushion all the time I was there. It sat in front of me like a dumb ox. I don't know, but I think I would have hit it if it was me. If that cushion could have been me, I would have pummeled it black and blue—well, that's easy to say afterward, isn't it—but probably all the time I wouldn't have hit it, even if it was me. But every time I had the cushion in front of me, Bala said it was my ma or my old man.

I didn't want to hit my old man. At the time I thought it was because I'd seen him crying, defeated, beaten by life. But after Bradley said that bit about on the run, then I knew I didn't want to hit him because he was already on the run. What good would it do to hit a man who's on the way down?

My ma I couldn't hit for other reasons—mainly, I think, because I loved her once and because she was a woman, a cheating woman, but still a woman. I don't know what diffs that makes, but I couldn't do it.

All I ever did with that cushion was collapse my head on it and lie there quietly, with my brain ticking away.

In a way, it was a quiet time for me in that Villa. Except for the last week I was there. That was when Bala's words started eating away at me like a caterpillar on a leaf.

In the beginning I spoke about things in South Africa in a distant sort of way. I think I didn't want to say anything in front of Bradley or Bala, who was from Sri Lanka. But after I was there four weeks, I got so used to talking in front of them all, and living and joking with them, that it became easier to talk about my South African life. That life seemed to come nearer and nearer. Perhaps it was from so much talking about it or because Bradley was interested in South Africa and what life was like there. Or because Bala kept on hinting that my childhood had something to do with how screwed up I was.

But in the last week things started getting too close for comfort.

It started getting awkward for me when I told them about the hair clip.

What happened was that Matilda, our servant girl (I had to explain to them that we called her a girl, but really she was thirty-something years old, and we called Alfred the garden boy, even though he must have been sixty-something years old)—well, anyway, Matilda was supposed to make our beds every day. It was one of her duties, like cleaning the house, making the beds, cooking the meals for us, and staying with us, that's Stelly and me, in the evenings when my folks went out and Lynette was off somewhere with one of her boyfriends. Matilda didn't have to do anything outside; that was Alfred's job.

Anyway, I told them, one day I caught her out lekker.

"Hey, Matilda, why you didn't make my bed properly today?"

"No, basie, I did it." *Basie* is a little master.

"Don't lie to me, hey. Look here, man, use your own eyes." I pulled the top sheet and blankets off. "What's that in the bed, hey? I'll tell you what it is. It's a hair clip, that's what it is. And I put it in there this morning before I went to school. And it's still there. Why's it still there, Matilda? You tell me."

"I don't know, basie."

"I tell you why, Matilda. It's because you didn't make my bladdy bed properly, that's why."

"Sorry, basie. I'll do it properly now."

"Now's too late, man. You do it properly every morning, see?"

It was Jane in the group who took offense to that

story. I told her not to get too worked up about it because most of the white kids in Joburg treat their servants like that; there was nothing at all unusual about it. But Jane thought it was terrible. She thought I was a slave driver. Hell, she ought to see some boer families, I said; then she'd know how some people treat black people. I nearly was going to use that word *kaffir* because that's what some boers call black people. But, like I said before, I've always found that word odious to use, so I didn't mention it. Even so, Jane was in a fury.

Of course Kevin backed her up because he liked Jane, and after that for a few days those two were always picking on me. Over lunch one day, Jane said I was more messed up than I thought. And I said who was she to tell me that. (You know what she used to do? She used to cut the skin of both her arms to make heart shapes and other marks. It looked terrible. Her arms looked like they had a disease, but when you looked closer, you could see it was scabs and scars from cutting. I think she used sewing needles to do it with.)

Maybe I shouldn't have said that to her because Kevin then got himself all worked up, and we said a few vile things to each other, and he started to punch me, and I punched back, and soon we were rolling around on the floor.

By the time Bala broke it up, my lip was bleeding. But you know what? After that scrap, Jane and Kevin were okay to me. And I felt a bit better. At the next group, Bala asked Kevin why he used me instead of a cushion. And Kevin didn't have an answer. Then Bala said maybe I *wanted* to be used as a cushion.

"Why?"

"Maybe you want to be punished for what you did," Bala said.

Man, that got me sweating. It was definitely getting too close for comfort. How did he know that I had done something? I had never mentioned anything about killing anyone. Not to anyone. Ever.

That Bala is a funny chap. Sometimes I think he really has life figured out, but at other times I think he could do with a spell of living in the Villa, I mean a Villa for adults.

Sometimes he gets his teeth into something you say, and he pulls on it like a terrier until he gets what he wants. He was like that when I mentioned my bar mitzvah.

"Tell us about that, Selwyn."

"It was just when I was thirteen, and Jewish blokes have to become a man. Like they circumcise Jewish boys when they're born, and when they're thirteen, they have bar mitzvahs."

"But what did you have to do to become a man?"

"Nothing really. Just read from the Bible in *shul*—that's a synagogue. Actually not read. I had to sing it. For a few months, the rabbi taught me every afternoon at the Hebrew school to sing my bar mitzvah piece. And then in the evening I had to make a speech to the guests."

"Did you enjoy it?"

"Not the singing. I was scared. And not the speech either because it was phony. I had to say now that I'm a man I will blah, blah, blah, but I didn't feel like a man. I still felt thirteen. But I enjoyed the presents. All these people came up to me that I hadn't seen since Ouma Fanny's funeral, and they shoved checks in my pocket and said *mazel tov*—that's Yiddish for 'congratulations'."

Susan asked me how much money I made.

"A lot," I said. "There were over three hundred guests at that reception, and they gave me twenty or forty rands for a present, and some uncles even gave me a hundred rands, and my oupa gave me five hundred."

Susan said I was too rich.

"Ja, but the reception cost a lot of money, don't forget. It was in a smart Joburg hotel."

Susan then told us about the Kwakiutl Indians. She said they've got a ritual they call potlatch. And the chief throws a party, and he invites all the tribes in the area and to every person he gives a present or he burns a present in their honor, the biggest present he can afford. It costs him a fortune to throw the party, but that way he can show he's very rich and powerful.

Susan liked being a downer, but I could see what she meant. Everyone in Joburg did that. Each person had to have a bigger potlatch than the last one. And my older sister Lynette's wedding was just the same. That was the last time our family was together for an occasion.

"What do you mean?" Bala asked.

"She married Ross, who is Australian, and went with him to Adelaide. She was lucky because she left the country three months before . . ."

"Before what?" the terrier said.

Jeez, I had nearly lifted the cork off the bottle! My head started buzzing like a blue-arsed fly to think of a way out.

"Before my old man first thought of leaving South Africa. Before his business started going to the dumps."

The terrier still wasn't finished with me.

"Why didn't you feel you became a man?"

"Because at the reception I had to dance. And I hated it because I didn't know how to dance. And I shamed myself with the girls who were there. So afterward I asked Lynette to teach me her latest dances."

"Did that make you a man?" the terrier said.

"No."

Then Bala got out of me the story of Spin the Bottle and how I only kissed the tip of Kerren's finger and then he probed out of me the business about Matilda and the Greek statue.

At the time I was about twelve, Matilda had to stay in the house in the evenings to baby-sit for me and Stelly. I was twelve, but it was still called baby-sitting. Lynette hardly ever did any baby-sitting, and when she did, she spent all her time with her latest boyfriend in the lounge with the door shut. But usually she was out every night.

Matilda couldn't stay in her room if she was baby-sitting because her room was separate from our house. It was around the back by our shed. She had a little room there with a concrete floor that was polished red, and she had a bed in that room, and she put the legs of the bed up on bricks; I don't know why to this day. She was also allowed to use the garden tap around the back of the shed if she wanted to wash.

She lived there alone because her children had to live four hundred miles away in the homeland, like I said before. Her husband wasn't allowed to live there with her—he worked in another town. But sometimes in the morning we used to see a black man sneaking off out of her room and making a beeline down the drive before Sweetie woke up. And I don't think it was often the same man sneaking out of her room. She had lots of different men who would spend the night there. My old man didn't like it at all and used to warn her about it, but that sort of thing never stopped. He used to genuinely believe that Africans have different morals from white people.

Anyway, when she was baby-sitting she used to sit in the kitchen all night because she wasn't allowed to sit any where else in the house because that was for white people, not servant girls.

But one night when Stelly had gone to sleep, I had a bath, and after the bath I got this idea. I got down an encyclopedia, and I found this picture of a Greek statue, which had only a piece of cloth around its private parts. And I did the same to myself with a white towel.

Then I walked into the kitchen like that.

"Hey, Matilda," I said, showing her the picture. "You know what this is?"

"No, basie, what is it?"

"It's a picture of a Greek statue. The man had a towel around him just like me."

Then I showed her the picture of the Greek lady statue, and her towel didn't cover her tits or anything.

"Let me see if you can be like a Greek statue, Matilda. Here, I got a towel for you."

Matilda took the towel and put it around her, but on top of her smock.

"No, Matilda, you must do it like the statue, man. No clothes."

"No, basie. I'm too fat. I can't do that, basie, please."

Anyway, when she wouldn't do it, I ran out of the kitchen and I dropped my towel on the way, by accident on purpose, and my white arse must have been there for her to see.

I never told that story to anyone before, and after I told it, I wasn't sure that I should have. It made me feel a bit shameful. But the group listened and, apart from one or two witty comments, they didn't say anything bad to me.

That day Rosalie came to visit me. She didn't bring me anything, but it was nice of her to come, wasn't it?

She asked me if the Villa was okay and how did I get my cut lip and I told her.

And I told her what Bradley said about being on

the run, and I asked her if she knew what I meant. And she said so many people who leave South Africa are exiles—that was what she called them—and maybe all exiles are on the run.

"South Africa does crazy things to people," she said. "Have you ever thought what a crazy life it was?"

"I never did until this week," I said.

"It's a cruel place," she said. "There's a lot of blood there and a lot of pain."

That night I had a bad, bad dream. I woke up poep-scared and shaking and sweating.

You know what I dreamt? I was walking somewhere near Ellis Park Stadium, and this bomb had gone off and people were running in all directions. I checked the time on this watch I had on my wrist that my old man gave me for a birthday present. It cost him a hundred and fifty rands wholesale. There was smoke everywhere from the bomb, but through it I could see this black woman who looked a bit like Matilda sitting on an upside-down bucket and breast-feeding her baby. Then this tsotsi about my age comes running toward me. He's running from the bomb, but I know he wants my watch and I think: The bogger, let's see what he will do. So I took the watch off my wrist and I just carry it in my left hand, not hidden in my fist, but sort of hanging down so he can see it. And the tsotsi runs past me, and suddenly I feel the watch pulled from my hand. I turn around, and the tsotsi is running like hell. I chase after him. And I'm stamping my feet on the ground to make as much noise as I can. And I'm feeling very fit from playing lots of rugby at school, so I think I can catch up to him. "You fokking bastard!" I'm shouting. "I'm going to moerra you, you bastard!" And he gets scared and he looks around and I'm nearly catching up. So he drops the watch. But I keep running after him. And I catch him and throw him to the ground, and I stamp on his face with my shoes. And there's blood coming from his face and he's screaming, "Eina! Eina!" but I don't stop until he stops screaming. And then I look down and he's dead. And I know his face. It's Philemon Majodena, and I've killed him. And the woman who looks like Matilda comes walking with her baby and she says to me, "Sis, basie, shame; you shouldn't have done that." And I look up at her, and she has a kind face, and the baby she is carrying is a white baby with blond hair and a triangular nose.

Chapter 8

"Is she your girl friend?"

Kevin and Jane were curious about my friendship with Rosalie. They were both a lot nicer to me after the scrap.

"No, she's the daughter of a friend of my ma's."

"But do you like her?"

"I don't know. I haven't thought about it."

I had. A lot. Rosalie was really nice, do you know what I mean? She had lovely brown eyes and wavy hair. Her arms were soft; she kept her fingernails neat and just a bit pointed; and yes, she had a lovely body—and I used to spend a lot of time thinking what it would be like if she let me feel her.

Or if she let me kiss her. I didn't know if I would be shy with her or what. Maybe I would just freeze up. Mind you, it was a long time since I last froze up about anything. Maybe it was the tablets they were giving me at the Villa.

"Have you ever shown her your white arse?" Kevin asked me.

That made me cross.

"I didn't tell you that story for a joke, you know," I said.

"Sorry, only teasing."

I told the group about my dream, but I pretended none of it had any connection with the truth. I pretended I'd never heard of Philemon Majodena, and I wish I hadn't.

I told them the dream had something to do with Joycie Adams. She was our servant girl in Cape Town, from the time I was born until the time I left there, when I was seven. She was a colored. That means something different from what it means in England. It means she wasn't black and she wasn't white, but a mixture. According to Mr. Jongsma, my geography teacher in Joburg, that's why she had no teeth in the front of her mouth because if you mix races, it's not so good for your body because of the degeneration of the genes. He also said that's why they have to be careful in South Africa when they do heart transplants because it's no good if a white person gets the heart from a black person, and vice versa is true also. That's what this teacher said, and I told the group.

"If you believe that, you must be nuts," Jane said.

Joycie Adams was nice. My ma used to play a lot of tennis when she was young—competitive tennis. And with all the socializing, she was away a lot of the time. Joycie was nanny for me and Lynette, and we were with her all of the time, except when my ma gave us a special treat like taking us to the beach at Muizenberg or to Kirstenbosch Gardens for a picnic.

I can't speak for Lynette, and I've never asked her, but Joycie was like a ma to me. She looked after me like I was her baby. I think that's why the baby in the woman's arms in my dream was white. It was me.

"So the woman was like a mother to you?" Bala said.

"Ja, she was."

I told them lots of white people in South Africa had the same thing with their nonwhite nannies.

"How long was she a mother to you?" Bala asked. I told you he never gave up on a subject until he was happy.

"I don't know. Until I left Cape Town. But when we got to Joburg, then we got Matilda and she wasn't a mother to me, no way. It was only Joycie Adams who was."

Then we were back onto the subject of Matilda again, and I decided to tell about the chocolates. I knew that telling these personal things pleased Bala because he thought I was opening up about myself. I reckoned as long as I could keep him happy this way, he wouldn't notice my bloodstained tracks.

This chocolates business was something that

used to happen quite a lot when I was thirteen or fourteen.

I used to tell Matilda to go buy me chocolates.

"Hey, Matilda. I want you to go to the shops today, okay?"

"Yes, basie."

"You get me one Crunchie and one Milky Bar, okay?"

"Yes, basie."

"Here's two rands. You bring me the change, okay?"

"Yes, basie."

"And don't take all afternoon to walk to the shops!"

"No, basie."

"And when you come back, you put the Crunchie and the Milky Bar and all the change here on my desk, okay?"

"Yes, basie."

While she was walking to the shops, I used to have a bath and then I would go into my room and lie kaalgat on the bed (that translates as "naked hole," but I suppose it just means "naked"), except for a small towel hanging over me and not hiding the fact that I was rigid with anticipation. The bed was right next to my desk, and Matilda had to put the Crunchie and the Milky Bar and the change on that desk, while I just pretended to be asleep.

After this had been going on a while, Matilda was fired from her job by my old man. He told me that she was too sick with heart trouble to work anymore. And we got another servant girl, whose name was Violet. But I didn't do that sort of thing with her because when I was fourteen, the thing happened with Philemon Majodena, and I didn't do anything else after that.

I didn't tell the group that. They would have asked me what happened with Philemon Majodena, and I didn't want to tell them that I killed him. And Bala would have gotten his teeth into me and pulled out the truth. They would have asked me too many questions, and I didn't want to talk about it anyway. It was none of their business what happened to him.

"My old man fired Matilda," I said. "But he used to go to Sun City with my ma twice a year for a long weekend, and there they used to gamble and watch black women doing striptease and dancing kaalgat."

Even the Afrikaners used to do the same thing. Go for a dirty weekend in Sun City or Swaziland. As long as it wasn't in South Africa proper, you could get a dirty weekend at a smart hotel, with gambling and a banned, uncensored film and a black woman thrown in at a bargain price. That's what I heard, anyway. In South Africa itself, most people thought it was a crime for black men and white women or white men and black women to go together. I don't think my ma had her eyes on black men in those days, although you never know. But just let her loose in England, hey, and she makes up for those years in double-quick time.

The second to last day I was there, I was called in for an interview with Dr. Richards, the psychiatrist. I had one interview with him each week. He's the one who says what goes on at the Villa, but I've never gotten on his wavelength, and anyway, once a week for an hour isn't a lot.

At the end of that interview, he asked me if I was ready to go home. I said yes. He said he thought so, too, that I'd come a long way. I wanted to tell him the only long way I'd come was from South Africa. I didn't really fancy going home, but home had one advantage—nobody would ask me questions for a while. I told you Bala's questions were beginning to eat me like a caterpillar.

My last day at the Villa they gave me a party. There were some Cokes and sweets and nuts and chips in bowls and a good-luck card.

The way everyone was hogging the sweets made me think of one last thing to tell them about South Africa.

About three or four times, I went from Joburg to Cape Town with my family for a holiday by train instead of going in the car (because it's a long way). We used to sit in these all-white carriages and watch the view. And we passed through lots of stations on the way. Some were only small places that had three houses and a church and a station and that's all. And some places were bigger towns, with the African townships outside, where the black people lived.

All along the route there were these piccanins. Some were just naked or standing in broken shorts or a broken dress, and they used to wait by the train line for presents.

I used to have a whole pile of sweets in wrapping papers ready to throw out of the train window one at a time. And these piccanins used to stand there with their hands begging, "Please, baas! Please, baas!" If you ever threw a candy, about four or five piccanins would go running after it to pick it up, and they would squabble like ducks trying to get a piece of bread.

One time the train stopped at this siding, and there was a police station there with a fence between the garden of the police station and the train line. And there were piccanins lined up by that fence with their hands begging. So I threw one-cent coins, about six of them, into the garden of the police station, and the piccanins had to climb the fence to get them.

When I told that story, I knew that Jane and Kevin would think it was outrageous. They would feel sorry for the piccanins. At that time in South Africa, I actually thought I was giving them presents. They looked so thin and hungry to me, I wanted to give them something. I even imagined the piccanins would think I was generous. Throwing those coins into the police station was just a bit of fun, I used to think. But when I told the story that last day in the Villa, I wasn't so sure of my actions anymore. I felt bad about it, and I said so to the group. They all gave me three cheers for feeling ashamed about something on my own, without comments from them to help me along.

Actually, I didn't just feel ashamed. If some bloke threw one-cent coins for *me* into a police station, I would think he needs his head examined. Like Rosalie said, South Africa makes people crazy.

The good-bye card they gave me was okay. I thought of starting a collection of these big cards that everybody signs. But at least these okes at the Villa said what they meant. *Don't give in to the bastards,* Kevin wrote. *You're okay,* Jane wrote. *Everyone at the Villa knows you've got guts,* Bala wrote. *You've proved it to us, and you can do the same outside.*

Chapter 9

As soon as I got home, I knew it was a mistake. I felt the waves getting bigger. Low tide was over. Soon it would be high tide again, and those huge bogger waves would come crashing over me again.

I felt it as soon as I got in the house. It smelled of phoniness. My ma was pretending to be nice. She had baked my favorite cake—banana cake with thick icing—and made a tasty spread for me with chocolates and chips and nuts and sweets. But I couldn't eat much because of the farewell party at the Villa. My ma and my old man both forced themselves to say how nice it was to have me back again, and

Stelly had made a WELCOME HOME sign. She was the only genuine thing in that house, I reckoned.

Even in the car on the way home I could smell two things: whisky and my ma's perfume. The whisky was on my old man's breath. And in the house I could smell it again. I hadn't even been home an hour before I saw my old man sneak into the lounge and secretly pour himself a large whisky. My ma was looking daggers at him.

Back in Joburg the liquor cupboard was always locked, but even then sometimes the liquor was stolen. It must have been Matilda, though we never caught her at it, but you could tell from the bottles that someone had been drinking the contents. And she did often look a bit merry.

But the worst one with drinking was Jubilee. He worked for my old man at the food warehouse. Sometimes he used to come in after lunch like he didn't know if he was Arthur or Martha. Eyes bloodshot, rocking on his feet like a rocking horse, and with a sheep's smile on his face.

"Kom hierso, Jubilee," my old man would say. (That means "come here.")

"Ja, baas?"

"You been bladdy drinking again, kaffir!" (My old man did sometimes use that word when he was very angry.)

"No, baas, I haven't."

"Don't lie, man. I can smell it a mile off. It's that bladdy kaffir beer."

"No, baas. I haven't been drinking. Only Seven Up."

"Seven Up, kak, man! I'm not paying you to come here drunk. No money today. You can bladdy go now. You are becoming a dronkie, you know that? Listen, man, if this happens one more time, Jubilee, it's finished. Verstaan jy?" (That means "Do you understand?")

"Ek verstaan, bass. Ja, ek verstaan."

"Nou ja, voetsek. And don't bother to come in tomorrow unless you're one hundred percent sober."

My old man never fired Jubilee because he was good at his job when he was sober. He used to make up all the orders in the stockrooms and stack up all the sugar and mielie meal and flour bags, and he used to do a lot of the deliveries in the big van. He did it for twenty-seven years with the previous owners of the business, and he worked nine more years for my old man. But when he was drunk, he was useless, my old man said, because he didn't even know his own name.

During that first week at home, I could see that my old man was getting like Jubilee. He didn't work till ten o'clock at night anymore. He was home between five and six. He never said why, but I knew his business was in trouble. And so was his marriage. And his old man was dead. I don't know if he missed Oupa like I did, but he started to look really old like Oupa. Big bags under his eyes and his head much balder in the front and in the middle.

Ma just ignored him most of the time. And she went out more than ever. I never saw her with the black man again. For all I know, she had someone new to prance around with.

When I turned up at school the day after I got back, the guys looked at me like I was a ghost, like the way those people must have looked at my old man when he walked out of the elevator alive after falling three stories.

They hardly knew what to say. Jeez, they looked frightened almost. I think my turning up gave them a skrik.

"Did you like the Mario Brothers?"

"Who were they?" I asked.

"The game we sent you in the hospital."

"Oh, that. Yes," I lied.

"Will you be playing soccer again?"

"Ja, I guess I'll give it a go."

"Wha? Wha did you say?"

Oh, cripes, man, why can't these guys listen?

I skipped school the next day and went to sit by the gorge. It was fantastic there. I liked that gorge. It was the only place I knew in England that was good. It was like the sanctuary for me.

The suspension bridge was old, and I don't like old buildings—all the buildings in Joburg are brand new. I mean, there's nothing there more than a few years old; then they tear it down and build something new. But I liked the suspension bridge and I liked Brunel for building it. You know what his first names were? It's written on his bridge on a plaque. I'll tell you. Isambard Kingdom. No, I'm not kidding. It's the dinkum truth. It sounds like an African name, like Jubilee, but I don't think it was.

That night my ma and my old man argued like mad, behind their closed bedroom door. My ma was swearing at my old man for drinking and for letting his work go to pieces, and he was swearing at her for gallivanting all over the place. That was his word for doing something bad—*gallivanting*—and it made me think he knew what my old lady was up to in her spare time.

Then I heard a loud falling noise, and I was glad at least that my old man had left his revolver in Joburg. Because in the old days, if I had heard a noise like that, it would have made me worry that things were getting violent and that any moment my old man could pull out that gun and use it on somebody. He did leave it in Joburg, didn't he? Didn't the police take it from him? Or did he sell it or something? Hey, man, there was a hole in my memory, and I couldn't figure out what actually happened to that blasted revolver.

They went on screaming for hours, and I thought, jeez, I wouldn't like to be living in the house squashed up against us next door. It must have kept them up all night.

But I didn't hear this arguing; you know why? I put earplugs in my ears made out of cotton, and I ducked my head under the blankets like I used to duck when we drove past cemeteries when I was younger.

And the next day I went back to the gorge and I sat there. And while I was sitting there, I saw something I never saw in my whole life before. I'll never forget it 'cause it gave me a helluva shock.

I wouldn't have seen it if someone hadn't started shouting on the suspension bridge. I looked that way. There were a few people shouting and pointing at a man who had climbed up on the wire railings right in the middle of the bridge.

Jeez, I got a skrik. The guy was going to jump. He was going to commit suicide right in front of everybody's eyes. I stood up to get a better view. And then he jumped. My heart stopped beating, you know. I got such a shock. It's not the sort of thing you see every day, is it?

Man, that guy fell a long way. Jeez, never mind an elevator shaft. That was like ten elevator shafts, one on top of the other. It was just like when I took the overdose and I started falling into the center of the earth. Except there was no way this oke was going to survive his fall. Down, down, down, down! I tell you, everything stopped in the world for those moments while he fell. Nothing seemed to move. Except for his body. Down, down, down, down!

Down in the bottom of the gorge is this river. It's called the Avon. And when it's full, it looks like a river, but when the tide is out, it looks like a bath of mud with a trickle of water in the middle, like those spruits you get in South Africa that have bridges over them and they're so dry you've got to guess where the river would go if it rained.

Anyway, the tide was out that day, and this oke was heading down, down, toward the mud. Jeez, what a way to go. Dropping like a bullet into thick, oozy mud. And he was nearly at the mud, just a bit farther to go, and I'm sure he would have disappeared into that mud completely, like a stone when you throw it at some mud and it just sinks in, no trace.

But you know what happened? I couldn't believe it. When he was right near the mud, he started going up again! Back up toward the bridge! Talk about miracles, I thought. Talk about falling through a wooden trapdoor! Talk about walking on water! This oke was being flown up again to the bridge, being saved from certain death.

I think a lot of things snapped in my brain when I witnessed that miracle because I thought the world must have different laws from what we were taught at school. Talk about the law of gravity! This guy was floating up—completely against the law of gravity.

But then I saw the rope. He was sort of joined by a rope to the bridge. Then I realized it was an elastic rope, a huge elastic rope, and this guy was pulling a stunt. He must have been a stunt man, I thought.

Afterward, when he was arrested by the police, I asked someone what was happening, and they told me this oke belonged to a society for doing daring sports.

Jeez, I've never heard of such a thing. Talk about a domkop! What if his elastic broke? Or if it stretched a few meters longer than he expected?

That night I wrote the first poem in the pad Rosalie gave me. I used the new pen. I found myself deep in the underground mine, drilling at the rock face with a light on my helmet and sweat pouring down my face. And then the rocks with the gold veins were transported in little railway trucks to the workshop, where they were crushed in huge machines and tipped into vats. As the furnaces reached their highest temperatures, I could see the rich yield from the earth. There were shining stripes in the rocks, veins of gold, and some of those veins were the stripes of phantom tigers prowling on the edge of a gorge, and in other veins were images of an oke jumping into a chasm with only a bit of elastic to save him from certain death, and there was a rondavel—that's a round hut with a straw roof—on the summit of the gorge where explorers could rest for the night, and the rondavel was called the Villa, and inside that rondavel, around a burning fire, the explorers told each other tales of the day's adventures, and there was a girl there, who came in the middle of the night when it was pitch black, and she took one of the explorers by the hand, and she said she knew about the waves breaking on the beach, that she had been thrown by them and battered by them, but that now she wanted to ride them like a surf rider, and why didn't he come away with her? And the rocks containing the precious mineral were melted in those fiery furnaces, and the steaming gold ink was poured into the inkwells, and I used my new pen to write that poem.

It was a poem for Rosalie.

I wrote it in my best handwriting on the first page of that pad, and I wanted her to see it. I wanted to contact her, there and then at two-thirty in the morning, and say, "Come over, man; I've got something to show you. It's for you." But I didn't I waited until the next day.

I spent that day also at the gorge, and I backed

out of contacting Rosalie, but when I came home late in the afternoon, there was trouble. My old man was waiting for me.

"Where've you been all these days?" he said.

"What's it to you?"

"I'm your father. That's what it is to me!"

"You're not like a father anymore."

"Don't cheek me, Selly. I'm not in the mood for it."

I could smell the whisky on his breath.

"I know you haven't been going to school," he said. "Your headmaster's been on the phone to me."

"So? I don't like that school."

"But where have you been going, man?"

"Nowhere important."

"Don't play stupid with me, Selly. I want to know."

"Okay. I've been going to the gorge in Clifton."

"Don't lie to me, man! I know where you've been going."

"Where?" I was amazed that he knew where I was going all those times.

He turned around and pulled something off the sideboard. It was a book. It was my bladdy pad! The one Rosalie gave me! The one with the poem on page one. My love poem to Rosalie! The bastard, how did he get hold of that, snooping in my room and reading my private poems?

"Give it to me!" I shouted, trying to take it back. "That's private. It's not for your drunk eyes."

Jeez, I was mad. I struggled with him, but he was strong and he wouldn't give me my pad back.

"I'm right, hey? Who's the bitch you've been seeing?"

Hell, I was thankful at least that I hadn't written Rosalie's name anywhere. At least he didn't know that.

"Man, have you got her pregnant or what?"

Bladdy hell, was he on the wrong track! Where did he get that idea from?

"Give that pad to me. It's mine."

"Ja, you want to get rid of it, hey? Because it's evidence."

What was the matter with him? Shit, the dronkie had misunderstood the poem, that's what!

The poem was about love and feelings between people and reaching into each other to find the gold liquid of love. And my bastard old man was thinking it was about sex and making someone pregnant!

"Give it back to me! I don't want to get rid of it. It's mine. I just don't want you to have it."

And then you know what the bogger did? He ripped that first page out of the book and gave the pad back to me. But the page with the poem he scrumpled up and shoved in his dirty pocket.

You can imagine I went wild.

"I haven't been seeing a girl. You've got it all wrong! Just like with Ma! Can't you see what she's been up to? It's not me who's getting someone pregnant. You go ask her. . . ."

I never got the next sentence out of my mouth. His fist came down on my jaw like a mountain of bricks. I thought my jaw had been smashed open like a tomato hitting a wall. It felt terrible. I just lay there on the floor, collapsed.

My old man turned around and went up to his room.

I just lay there on the floor.

I thought, it's true; that man's on the run. He's never once spoken to me about Philemon Majodena, even though it was *his* bladdy revolver that shot the boy. He's been running from that boy's blood so fast, he can't see he's headed for a rock face. When he hits it, he's going to smash worse than my jaw.

Chapter 10

The next day I phoned Rosalie and asked her to meet me in the café at the antiques market in Clifton after school.

"Your lip's better," she said. "But what's happened to your cheek now?"

My cheek was bruised.

"My jaw's aching all over," I said.

I told her about the row I'd had with my old man the previous day. And I apologized for not having a copy of the poem to give her.

"I tried to write it out afterward," I said, "but I was in too much pain to remember it all properly."

"Never mind," she said. "You can write me another one someday."

"Ja, I will."

"But you can't go on living there with your father so violent with you."

"He's just going through a bad time," I said.

"You should get away from there."

"Where to?" I asked.

"What about back to the Villa?" she said.

"Ag, I don't know."

"Hey, what about . . . I've got an idea. It's just one weekend, though."

"What's the idea?"

"Come with me to Dorking, to my dad's place. It's nice. It's in the country and it's peaceful and it will give you time to think where you want to live. What do you think of that idea?"

"My old man won't like it. He'll think I'm off with a girl."

"This time you are. But does he have to know?"

"Maybe I can just tell my ma," I said. "She knows your ma."

"Why don't you leave it to me? I'll suggest it to my mom. I'll tell her you need a rest, and it will be good for you at Dad's place. And I'll ask her to arrange it with your mother. They'll think they're doing a good thing. And then let your mother explain it to your father."

"We can give it a try."

My old man was too drunk to know what was going on anyway. He didn't go to work the day after he hit me or the day after that. And then it was the weekend. He didn't even see me go.

My ma said it was okay with her. She liked Rosalie, and Ginny had persuaded her that Rosalie's dad wouldn't mind.

We took the train from Temple Meads after Rosalie finished school on Friday.

The house was near Dorking, not in Dorking, on the side of a hill. Mr. Morris told me it was the Downs. I liked him and couldn't understand at all why Ginny had divorced him. He had a beard and moustache all in one, which was not exactly grey and not exactly black, but somewhere mixed between the two. His left eye was squint or something, or maybe it was a bit blind. But he was very cool about everything. By cool I don't mean he was trendy or cool in that way. He was just cool, like he didn't get ruffled by things. That's how he seemed, anyway. It surprised me that a man who had been in jail and locked away in solitary for so long could be so calm. I think if that was me, I'd have lost my marbles.

He kissed Rosalie hello and he shook my hand, and after that, we didn't see that much of him the whole weekend, except once or twice and at mealtimes.

He had lots of visitors drop in and a couple of guests who spent the whole weekend there. One of the guests was a woman, Irma Crossley; the other one was a man, who I just knew as James. Rosalie told me that Irma was a well-known actress who campaigned against apartheid, and James was a lawyer. I think he was working for the ANC (that's African National Congress, the organization that's fighting against the South African government). But he didn't speak to me much the whole weekend.

I don't know what they all did that weekend, but Mr. Morris is a busy man. He wasn't just a member of Anti-Apartheid like Jeff's folks. He works full-time to change South Africa, one way or another; that's what Rosalie told me.

I must admit I was a bit frightened to be in a house with those sort of people. Of course, the South African government would have called them communists, but I didn't know if they were real communists or not. Still, the idea made me feel jumpy. What if they were planning sabotage or bombs in Joburg or something like that, or if the South African security police should raid the house? But being with Rosalie was so good, it was worth the risk.

For sure that weekend we spoke for more hours together than I've ever spoken with anyone else in my life. We spoke nearly all the time, except when we were eating and sleeping and . . . well, I'll tell you about that later. First things first, hey?

Mr. Morris had a good library in that house. It had all sorts of books: poetry and novels and ency-clopedias and books on politics. There were even some books by Karl Marx. I'm sure those would have been banned in South Africa. There was a couch in that library and a big swivel chair with a leather seat. There was leather on the desk also, and lots of papers and things. I think Mr. Morris was in the middle of writing books or articles on South Africa. But we didn't go near those papers. Mostly we sat near each other on that couch or else we sat in the garden on a bench near the hedge, where we could see the Downs going up behind the house. It's a silly name for hills, isn't it, Downs? I mean they should be called Ups. Anyway, we could see the hills from where we sat in that garden.

We talked about everything. She told me what it had been like for her when her dad was arrested in South Africa. The security police came for him at dawn. They completely ripped apart his whole study, pulling out all the drawers from his desk and his filing cabinets. They made a mess of all his papers and documents and took away box loads as evidence. He was rushed away in a police van without any mention of where he was going. It took Ginny a few days before she found out that he was in prison and would stay there indefinitely, without a trial even. Rosalie said it was the worst moment of her life because she was eleven when it happened, and she knew the police were hurting her dad in the jail. In the beginning, they beat him up day and night, and that damaged his left eye. She said they wanted him to sign a document about the other people involved in whatever he was doing.

"Did he sign it?" I asked.

"Yes. He couldn't take the torture. But they didn't break his spirit."

I asked what he had been doing. I thought maybe it was making bombs or something, but Rosalie said no, he was just helping with a newspaper because he was a journalist.

Even when the South African government deported Mr. Morris, they didn't tell his family. They just took him to a plane and put him on it. He phoned them from England, and that was the first they knew. Ginny had to sell their house and their possessions, and she and Rosalie flew to England to be with him.

At first they were so glad to see him again, but he had changed a lot also. Rosalie said he was filled with anger and wanted to get even with South Africa and spent all his time writing and going to meetings. Within twelve months, he and Ginny were divorced. It was like Oupa—he couldn't stand the move either. Except that Oupa had lasted less than two months and died a stranger in a strange land.

That was another bad time for Rosalie, but she said her mom was a strong person and made a new life for them in Bristol. A new life, nothing to do with politics. That was about three years ago. Mr. Morris didn't look full of anger to me. He looked really calm. Maybe that kind of anger doesn't show in a person's face, or maybe he wasn't so angry anymore.

For someone who said her life had nothing to do with politics, Rosalie sure knew a lot about the subject. One time on that weekend, she told me about some of the books on those shelves that she had read. Mostly books about South Africa, but also books on blacks in America and Martin Luther

King, and books on the slave trade. (She told me about those in lots of gory detail—did you know that more than half of the slaves on each ship that went to America died before they ever crossed the ocean? I didn't, and it shocked me.)

She also knew a lot about Jews and Nazi Germany, even though her family's not Jewish. That was very odd to me because even though I'm Jewish, I've never been interested in Jewish things. My ma didn't bring us up that way, and my old man was only Jewish in a superstitious way. The only time you knew our family was Jewish was at weddings, funerals, and my bar mitzvah. But some of the things Rosalie knew about the persecution of Jews were terrible. She showed me pictures of the Nazi concentration camps and of mass graves.

I told her about my oupa escaping from Poland, and then I also remembered my Great Aunt Freda, who lived in Krugersdorp with Uncle Frank. She had a number tattooed into her arm. That was done to her in the concentration camp in Germany. The only thing I remember about Great Aunt Freda was that she said she lived life to the full because she was so lucky not to die in the concentration camps, and she wanted to bring up her children the same way. But I had never thought about what she must have gone through. Yirra! It made my flesh creep to think about it.

The way Rosalie spoke about the Jews, I couldn't understand why Great Aunt Freda had servants in her house. If she knew firsthand about prejudice, how could she ever treat anyone like an inferior? But maybe she didn't; I don't know. I never knew her well. It really got me thinking, though, about my own family and about my old man being so frightened by the three-sided swastika of the Afrikaner extremists.

Sometimes when Rosalie talked about something, she got down a book from the shelves to show me. Some of them were written by black people, and it was the first time I ever touched such a book. She even showed me a little book of speeches or something by Nelson Mandela. She said if I wanted, I could borrow some of them; her dad wouldn't mind, but I felt a bit nervous about being caught with a banned book.

We talked a lot about prejudice and our own lives back in South Africa. And I told her some of the things I had managed to throw up at the Villa—about Matilda and how I used to treat her. And she told me similar stories about her servant girl Elsie. And sometimes while we were telling each other these things, we shook our heads sadly to think that we had been like that. And sometimes we laughed—but it wasn't funny. It was a kind of painful embarrassment because it was ourselves we were talking about.

I think I had to come to England to be able to talk about these things. If I had stayed in South Africa, I would never have thought such things, never in a million years. But sitting there with Rosalie, I began to feel the connections between all people and the stupidity of acting superior because of a skin color or religion.

Then we got onto what it must have been like to be a slave captured in Africa or a Jew in Nazi Germany or a black living today in South Africa, or in America, or in England, for that matter. I thought about Bala being from Sri Lanka and what it must be like for him, and about Bradley, who was on the run, and I wished I could meet him again so that we could both stop running, just turn around and face the hyenas on our tracks together.

Ja, I realized that not only was my old man on the run, but my ma also, with her gallivanting. And me, too. I was definitely on the run. Running without stopping to think. Without stopping to feel. Without stopping to feel the pain. But God knows where we were all running to. I wanted to stop running—and Rosalie said wanting to is half the battle.

We talked late into the night, till after midnight, and I held her hand, and I kissed it, and I held her, and I felt her body, and I kissed her on the mouth. It was fantastic the way she led me on.

But just when I was really getting into it, she dropped this bombshell on me. She told me about Justin. Who the hell was Justin, for God's sake?

It turned out Justin was this sixteen-year-old boy from Bristol who she'd been seeing for about a year.

"Is it over between you and him?" I asked.

"I don't know," she said. "We have our ups and downs, I suppose, but we've had good times together."

I could hardly say anything.

"So why did you bring me over here to Dorking, then?"

"Because you said you didn't know what to do, and I thought it would be nice to have you stay here."

"But you don't really feel anything for me, then?"

"Of course I do, Selly."

"But not like . . . you know, between a girl and a boy."

"I didn't say that," she said, snuggling up against me. "Let's see what happens between us."

Later we said good-night, but I found it difficult to go to sleep because of what she'd said. My first thought was to get the hell out of Dorking. It was dangerous at that house with all those activists there, and on top of it, Rosalie was just stringing me along. I was part of her do-good social work, that's all. She was like those Samaritans you could phone from the Clifton suspension bridge, trying to save me. But I didn't want her help; I just wanted her, plain and simple.

I would have sneaked out of the house there and then, but two things stopped me. First, I wasn't too keen on going back to Bristol. And secondly, I didn't want to run. I had to stop running. And to do that, I had to trust Rosalie. There was definitely something about her that was real. And anyway, maybe she was just boasting about this Justin character. Maybe she preferred me to him, who knows?

The next day we had a barbecue out on the grass with Mr. Morris and his friends. It wasn't the same as a South African braaivleis. It didn't taste the same. But it was nice to get the smoke in your eyes and to smell the meat braaing. There wasn't a swimming pool to jump into afterward, and anyway, it wasn't hot enough. It was one of those English summer days when the sun can't make up its mind whether it's worth the bother of shining or not. Still, I felt like I was with people who at least knew what a braai was supposed to be like, and everyone was very nice to me.

The odd thing, though, was this black lady, Thandi, who was visiting. She had arrived just before lunch, and I kept on having the feeling that I knew her or that she knew me. In some way she reminded me of Matilda. But Matilda would never in her wildest dreams have sat eating with us around the braaivleis.

She caught me looking at her once or twice and then came over to sit by me.

"I have two boys, teenagers just your age."

"Really?" I said.

"Ja, I miss them too much."

I looked closely at her sadness and thought she must also be an exile.

"They are just like you," she said. "But they are still in South Africa. They live with my cousin, but they're always in trouble."

"Are they?" I said, trying to picture what kind of trouble her two sons were in.

"Ja, this young generation is very bitter. They want to burn down everything that belongs to the white man."

"Aren't they afraid of the police?" I asked.

"It is difficult for you to understand. You have always had privilege. But my boys have had only the color of their skin. For them, it is freedom or death. They are not afraid of the white man's guns."

Eina! It nearly choked me when she said that. The food got stuck halfway down my throat. I ran inside to the toilet and put my fingers down my throat to let the air in. My eyes were watering and strings of saliva from my mouth dripped into the bowl. As I struggled for breath, this idea shifted into my head and wouldn't move. It was the idea that Philemon Majodena must also have had a mother.

From the toilet I went to the kitchen for a glass of water, and I stayed inside the whole afternoon until I thought Thandi had gone.

Later, Rosalie found me hunched up in the study. I was feeling really down in the dumps.

"Did Thandi upset you?" she asked me.

I was too bottled up to answer her.

"Are you upset with *me?*" she asked.

"I'm upset about everything," I grunted.

"It's because I mentioned Justin last night, isn't it?"

I was glad she changed the subject away from Thandi.

"Ja, you really shocked me."

"I'm sorry," she said. "I thought it was best you knew the truth before getting involved with me."

"Do you want me to get involved with you?"

"Of course I do," she said. "You know that. We understand each other really well. I want to get to know you better."

"What about Justin, though?"

"What about him? He doesn't take life seriously. I can't talk to him the way I talk to you."

Sometime that evening, Mr. Morris came into the study. He pulled down this old chocolate box from a top shelf and began to rummage through some photographs.

"How are you two doing? You haven't shown Selwyn the area, Rosalie. It's very nice around here."

"We're just talking, Dad," Rosalie said.

"She's quite a talker, isn't she, Selwyn?"

"She's also a good listener," I said.

"I agree with you there. I talk over lots of things with her that no one else would ever understand."

He found the photograph he was looking for and showed it to me. It was of a young African boy who couldn't have been older than nine, playing a guitar made out of an old oil tin. He was so proud of his guitar and the music he was making, he had this grin on his face from ear to ear.

"Do you miss South Africa, Selwyn, or haven't you been away long enough yet?"

"I miss it already," I said.

"So do I. But not the brutality," Mr. Morris said. "Not the inhumanity. Just the place. The smells. The feel of it all. The people. It's where our roots are."

After Mr. Morris went out of the room, Rosalie and I talked on into the night, beginning with roots.

"I wonder what such a lot of transplanting does to our roots," I said.

"I don't know," Rosalie said. "It takes a long time for roots to establish themselves."

"I wonder how deep roots go," I said.

"Your roots probably go back to Poland and Germany and even here in England."

"Maybe the roots go even deeper," I said, "to where we all come from, all human beings."

"That's really deep," she said.

"A human being must be a deep thing," I said. "No-man-fathomed."

Chapter 11

After midnight we were really getting into the swing of things again. Rosalie had convinced me that the situation with Justin was open, that for now she was with me and she liked me. And that it was equally up to me to help our relationship grow. Somehow I trusted her and felt safe exposing my real self to her. She didn't seem to mind all the scabby bits of my life. She had this knack of being able to look at scabs and see a whole lot of healing going on.

At about two in the morning, she asked me if I wanted to tell her about Philemon Majodena.

"Is it true that you killed him?" she said.

It shocked me when she asked; my insides started trembling. She would be the first person I ever told. But the words were locked so deep in me, I didn't know if they'd come out.

"Ja, I did. But I didn't mean to moerra him; you must believe me."

I told her that I never wanted to be a racist or a murderer. But I know I killed him, and it's my responsibility and my guilt, and I will always be guilty, and no one can take that away from me, even though I didn't go to court or anything.

"You don't have to tell me about it if it pains you," she said.

"I never speak about it," I said.

I bottled up, hugging my knees close to my chest to stop the shaking. But the memories were too vivid in my head, burning up my brain.

Then I told her about the night my old man's warehouse got burgled. At half past three in the morning, our phone rang. It was the police, to say the alarm at the warehouse had been set off again. It happened quite often. You know why? Because of rats. These rats used to come in for the flour and the mielie meal, and they used to climb along the alarm wires and set them off.

When we got called like that, the same thing always happened. My old man used to wake me up—I'm talking now about when I was thirteen and fourteen; I don't mean when I was younger—and I got dressed, and my old man used to take me along for the ride.

Usually we would get to the warehouse, and the

police were there, and my old man would let them in, and they'd all search around for a bit, and then they'd see rats or something.

But this one night we got there before the police, only a few minutes before. And my old man unlocks the front door and he goes in first, with me following behind. Now I didn't mention this, but he's got his revolver with him.

Well, my old man goes into the one stockroom at the back of the building, where the cold storage is, and I go into the other one, where all the mielie meal was kept. And as I got there, I caught a helluva fright. There was this black guy in there, climbing up the sacks of mielie meal to the high window. He had something in his hand, maybe a knife or a crowbar, or maybe it was a screwdriver. I just froze, but he jumped out the window.

And then I see this younger black chap hiding behind the mielie meal. He's more frightened than me, even. He's poep-scared, man. I could see his eyes looking up at me to see what I was going to do, and he was more terrified than the cat I tormented under the divan bed. That cat moaned with a man's voice, but this boy was just silent, and that cat tried to scratch its way out, but this boy was just still because he was petrified. And if I hadn't done anything, he would have just stayed there, and the police would have gotten him and locked him up. But I don't know why I did what I did; maybe it was my own fear or maybe I wanted to frighten him more, like terrorizing the cat that time under the divan bed, and I screamed out, "Monty!"

That scream made the boy move at last. He looked up at the window and made a jump for it.

"Monty! Come quick!" I yelled.

My old man comes running in. From the way I called him, he thinks I'm in trouble, and he comes to help me. He's pointing the revolver—I should have known he'd have it ready. And the boy is halfway in and halfway out the window. But my old man thinks the boy's on the way in, and he's going to attack me or something, and my old man wants to protect me, and he doesn't know this boy's unarmed, and then my old man shoots two shots. The noise is terrible! It cracks open the quietness of the night. And the boy jumps out of the window.

The police arrived soon afterward and they came into that stockroom and they opened the back door, and my old man tells them that there were two robbers, so the police go out after them both.

And the first one they find easily because he's lying in a pool of blood under the window where he jumped out, but the second one they never found.

And I looked at the boy, and he was dead. Man, he was my age—he couldn't have been a day older than fourteen, and his trousers were held up around his stomach with a piece of string, and he had these worn-out tennis shoes on his feet, and he was wearing a torn T-shirt, but it was soaked in blood, and his terrified eyes were still open, but they could see nothing anymore, and there was this river of blood that had flowed from his body and made a pool underneath him.

"I killed him, don't you think so?" I said.

I looked up at Rosalie. Her eyes were wide open, and she was staring at me. She didn't answer, so I went on.

I killed him because I called my old man into that stockroom, and I knew my old man had the revolver and he'd shoot if he saw anyone there. It wasn't my old man's fault. He couldn't have known that it was just a kid without any weapons, but I did, and still I called him, even though I could have just let that boy run away.

Ja, I killed him, and what he was doing in that warehouse I'll never know because what could he have stolen, you tell me. To do a good job of robbing a warehouse like that, you would need a truck, man. Two boys without a truck, what could they take? There wasn't even money in that warehouse. My old man had a safe in the other building, where the office was. Now *there* they could have taken money. But what were those okes doing in the warehouse?

His name was Philemon Majodena. I found that out later.

You know, the police just took down a statement from my old man. They thought it was a straightforward case—what did the boy expect if he went burgling? They didn't ask me anything. They didn't even see that I killed him also. I didn't even have to go to court.

I sat with Rosalie. She didn't say a thing. She looked at me, deep into my eyes, she held my hand, but she didn't say a thing, except "Shame, Selly." I think she also knew I was guilty.

We sat the whole night together. Not kissing or anything. Just sitting, holding hands, feeling the pain. We sat together the whole night, and when the dawn chorus started, we were still awake, and we walked outside.

We walked right up to the top of the Downs, and it was there Rosalie said that Philemon Majodena was a victim of the system. And I said to her that reminded me of Abraham and Isaac because Abraham took Isaac up to the top of the hill, and he said, "We're going to make a sacrifice to God here" and Isaac said, "Where's the animal we're going to sacrifice?" and Abraham said, "It's you! You're the bladdy sacrifice!" Talk about the victim of a system! Abraham was just damn lucky that the angel stopped him in time from killing his son. But no angel came to that warehouse for me. I wasn't stopped in time.

And from the top of the Downs we watched the brand-new morning start, and the green fields of England looked so beautiful in that fresh light, and we walked down again, through a field of cows.

And Rosalie saw one cow with something sticking out of her, so we went to take a closer look. And this cow was giving birth, right there and then. It took about five or six minutes.

The cow pushed once or twice, and this red bundle, looking like a package of meat from the supermarket wrapped in plastic, started to come out of the cow. More and more of the package got pushed out, and then it sort of slithered out all in one bundle. And it slithered out and dropped to the grass.

And the package of meat stood up, and it was a calf, complete with a head and four legs. And the mother cow turned around to lick its newborn, and the calf had black markings on its body and was walking its first few steps.

We watched that new creature until nine o'clock. The sun was shining, and it was time to go down for breakfast. And I looked at Rosalie, and I knew something had been born in me that morning. I told Rosalie this poem about i who was dead (that's supposed to be a small *i* because e.e. cummings wrote that poem). Anyway, i who was dead am alive again today, and this is the sun's birthday. And she said she liked that poem.

And we spoke more about victims. And I came to realize there was another victim that night in the warehouse. Me. Not a victim like Philemon Majodena. No, he got the worst of it, that's for sure. But still a victim in my own way.

I understood for the first time that besides the victimized—all those blacks who had died and were dying and suffering every day because of their skin pigment—there's also the victimizers—all of us whites who think we're the bee's knees, but really we're sleepwalking while a million scorpions crawl through our minds. South African scorpions are deadly, you know. One bloke I heard about in Joburg went to bed, and in the middle of the night he woke up screaming because something was crawling under him. This was in the middle of a Joburg suburb, not out in the bundu. Then he saw it, a small scorpion

—they're the worst—crawling from under his stomach. And he tried to brush it off, but it was too late. That deadly tail had already done its work. Ja, South African scorpions are bad.

Rosalie's eyes were shining in the sunlight. I looked at her, and I wondered again if she really cared for me or if she was just interested in me as someone she could help. Maybe she was only interested in trying to convert me to her beliefs. A sudden fear went through me that she was in fact a communist agent. Ag, no, surely not. That's the old paranoia coming back.

I looked at her eyes, and I wanted to believe that those eyes didn't belong to a communist or a noncommunist, a white or a nonwhite, a Jew or a non-Jew, a South African or an English or Polish person, a male or a female. I didn't want to be any of those things. I wanted to live forever in the place where a human being shines like gold liquid, in the place where the poems are made, where all our roots come from. I wanted to find that place in myself and in my old man and my ma and my dead oupa and Stelly and Lynette, and in Rosalie and Philemon Majodena, and Matilda and Bradley, if I ever met him again, and in Lloyd and John Patel.

And that morning the tigers were out on the Downs, savage golden animals, wild and magnificent and terrifying, and I saw them bounding across the chasms.

And I felt the rollers breaking on the shores of England, huge, sparkling waves with white manes that had the power to pick England up and throw it down in a different place or smash it to bits if they wanted.

And I didn't know what to think. I wanted Rosalie to like me. I wanted to stay with her, but I knew I couldn't stay at that house in Dorking. I had to leave, go back to Bristol maybe, to my father, who was disintegrating, and to my mother, who was trying to make it left, right, and center with everybody except my old man and me, and I didn't want to go back to them, although I felt sorry for Stelly being there all alone with them, but maybe I would have to go back. Maybe it would be different, now that I had a glimmering of understanding.

No, I knew I could not go back to them yet. Maybe I could go to the Villa, get myself into a better state. Give my old man some time to dry out and my ma some space to sort out her worries. I wanted to see Bala again, to talk to him, to feel his questions operating on me, opening me up.

And I didn't have a clue in hell where I was headed or what would happen to me now, and it was like this Irish monk I read about, who went out on the wild sea in a boat no bigger than a dinghy, and he said if this boat is destroyed by a storm, then that's it, but if it lands on a piece of rock, then that rock will be my home forever, and I sailed out into the middle of that wide ocean that joins South Africa to England to Poland to America to Germany to everywhere and everyone, and I waited to see where the winds would take me.